BADGERED TO DEATH

A WILDWOOD WITCH MYSTERY: BOOK 6

ELLE ADAMS

This book was written, produced and edited in the UK, where some spelling, grammar and word usage will vary from US English.

Copyright © 2022 Elle Adams
All rights reserved.

To be notified when Elle Adams's next book is released, sign up to her author newsletter.

With a family like mine, I expected my date night to get interrupted, but I didn't expect the instigator to be my grandmother's ghost. I was in the middle of the living room in my mother's house when I looked up and saw Grandma's transparent form waving cheerily from outside in the street.

Instead of waving back, I startled. I'd thought she was confined to my office, but she had been testing the limits recently and must have floated straight through the closed door to the Wildwood Coven's headquarters and out into the street.

"Oh no," I muttered as she pirouetted, her transparent feet skimming the ground. The only saving grace of having my grandmother's restless spirit take up permanent residence in my office was knowing I could at least get some privacy at home. From her, that was, since the rest of my family members were all too present in my life.

Crossing my fingers behind my back that she wouldn't be able to get *into* the house, I walked through the hallway and opened the front door. My red squirrel familiar, Tansy, ran past and hopped onto the garden wall to watch while I closed the door behind me and cleared my throat. "Grandma, what are you doing out here?"

"I thought I'd drop by for a visit." Her gaze fell to the neat front garden. "What *did* you do to my flowerbeds?"

"I didn't do anything," I told her. "If you have an issue with the garden, take it up with Mum."

"*And* you removed the black curtains?" She gave a sniff. "I can't believe you've forgotten me already."

Chance would be a fine thing. "The curtains made the living room look like a cave. Besides, you're still around, so we don't need to move on, do we?"

After my grandmother's death, the house had been decked out in mourning black in a manner that I found frankly excessive and that the woman herself had never appreciated in the slightest. This was the first time she'd even brought up the subject, but she gave me an affronted look and then shooed Tansy off the fence. "Did that familiar of yours *eat* my flowers?"

"Certainly not," Tansy answered in an indignant tone. "Your eldest daughter moved them into the back garden before the flower contest to keep them away from her sister."

"Exactly," I said. Tansy might have a taste for sunflower seeds, but she knew better than to snack on Mum's prizewinning flowers. On the other hand, my aunt Shannon had proven she wasn't above resorting to sabotage in order to win the town's annual flower contest, although my mother had come out the victor in the end. "Why not go to *her* house?"

"My youngest daughter is in disgrace," she returned. "I won't give her the honour of a visit."

Figures. Aunt Shannon had shown up the entire coven when her illegal potion-selling scheme had been publicly exposed, and I was willing to bet she was scheming for a shot at revenge on me for humiliating her. Since my aunt's house was right next door, it was nice to imagine Grandma floating in and catching her in the act, but I didn't need to encourage my grandmother's wandering tendencies any further.

"Fine." Instead, I paced down the road and beckoned to her to follow me. "C'mon. Let's go back to the office."

"Do not patronise me, Robin Wildwood." She folded her arms, a gust of wind stirring around her.

Oh man. Even a witch as powerful as my grandmother no longer had access to the magic she'd had when she was alive, but that didn't make her harmless. If she chose to blast off my mother's roof, for instance, I was pretty sure even my Head Witch sceptre wouldn't be able to stop her.

"I'm not."

A curtain twitched in the window of the house next door. *Great.* Aunt Shannon had come to watch the show.

"Mum doesn't have time to attend to your whims, and I thought you liked having the office to yourself."

Despite being dead, my grandmother refused to give up her old office. She wasn't going to let a little inconvenient incorporeality stop her from acting as if she was still Head Witch, and she'd refused point-blank to let me redecorate the place. It was bad enough having her hovering around me when I was working, let alone at home. I'd sooner camp out in the forest than have her for a roommate.

"Is your mother in the garden?" Grandma scoffed. "I'll go and sort her out."

She drifted purposefully towards the alley between Mum's house and its neighbour, but when she reached the opening, her body came to a sudden halt and jerked back as if she were at the end of a bungee cord that had reached its limit. With a huff of indignation, Grandma made a second attempt to get into the gap between Mum's house and Aunt

Shannon's, but her ghostly figure was unable to move any further.

I hid a smile of relief. *Good. She can't get into the house.* "Come on. You don't want someone leaving a pile of sage outside the office door when you're not around again, do you?"

"They wouldn't dare." She turned her back on the houses, her face a scowling mask. "I'll show them."

As Grandma finally began to drift back towards the coven's headquarters, Tansy cleared her throat from her perch on the garden wall. "We have company."

I followed her gaze and spied Harvey approaching. From the expression of utter bewilderment on his face, I assumed he'd witnessed a fair bit of my conversation with Grandma… except he lacked the ability to see ghosts, so it would have looked as if I was talking to myself.

"Erm." Why couldn't I get through a single day without my family showing me up? "Hey, Harvey."

"Hey, Robin," he said. "What's going on?"

"My grandmother's ghost went for a wander." I surreptitiously glanced at her retreating path, and I lowered my voice until I was sure she'd floated back into the coven's headquarters. "I was worried she'd get into the house."

His eyebrows shot up. "I thought ghosts were confined to a single location."

"You'd think, but you know how strong-willed she used to be when she was alive." I shrugged. "She's no different as a ghost."

I sometimes forgot most witches and wizards didn't have the ability to see ghosts because Grandma was such a demanding presence at headquarters that even the few coven members who couldn't see her knew exactly where she was at any given time. I had to admit I envied anyone who didn't have to listen to her throwing tantrums whenever I moved the furniture around the office so I could actually find the paperwork I needed.

"I bet." Harvey reached for my hand and pulled me in for a kiss, though he kept it chaste. "Should we go before she comes back?"

"Wise idea." I slid my hand into his as we made our way down the street, while Tansy scampered along at my heels.

"You didn't bring the sceptre?" Harvey asked, noting the absence of the large glowing stick I usually carried everywhere.

"No, Mum finally caved in." I'd argued that the sceptre was too cumbersome to carry around and painted a gigantic target on my head, and besides, it was safer in my bedroom than at the pub. "It's not like we're leaving town."

Rather, our destination was the Fox's Den, the local pub and our favourite date spot. Since it was run by shifters, my family weren't fans of the place, but in my view, they were missing out. The werewolf bartender gave us each a free drink on the house—a thank you for solving a murder a few weeks ago that had threatened their business—and had also reserved our favourite table by the window. Harvey and I settled down to order our meals and chatted while we waited for our food. I welcomed the cosy atmosphere as a balm to the stress of another week of Head Witch duties and navigating my family's many demands.

"Any plans for the rest of summer?" Harvey asked. "I should be done with classes in a few weeks."

"Then you'll start on the next school year of classes, right?"

Harvey was the captain of the local Sky Hopper team, and when he wasn't in the air himself, he was teaching classes at the academy. Since they'd broken up for the summer holidays, he'd switched to teaching summer school classes, but if anything, he was working longer hours than usual. Honestly, it was a miracle we had time to see one another at all, especially as the Head Witch didn't *get* a summer holiday.

"Yes, but I'll have a bit of free time in between."

Our meals appeared on the table in front of us.

He leaned forward. "You haven't said what your plans are. Aside from Head Witch stuff."

"My plans for the summer currently involve convincing my brother to spend more time with our dad"—I grabbed my fork and dug into my meal—"specifically, taking him to meet Jessica and the kids."

He lifted a brow. "How likely is it that you'll convince him?"

"Considerably lower than the odds of me shaking off this sceptre by Samhain."

"You never know. Haven't you been taking lessons from your grandmother?"

"When she isn't taking unexpected excursions." I ate a few more mouthfuls of delicious pasta.

The pub food might not be quite as good as Kimberly's, my family's chef, but it was the companionship I valued the most. My family didn't really hang out casually, except for the rare occasions I managed to convince my brother to sit down and watch a movie with me on one of his nights off.

Being surrounded by my overly competitive family for too long made it hard to tell if I was making any significant progress, though Harvey had a more optimistic outlook on my capabilities than I did anyway.

Harvey studied me for a moment. "*Is* there a chance you'll be able to give up the sceptre on Samhain? Even a small one?"

"Yes… in theory."

The last day of October was the official time for the appointment of a new Head Witch, though my own ascension to the position had been earlier due to my grandmother's untimely death. It also didn't mean I'd be freed on Samhain myself.

I waved my hand. "It depends if I've fulfilled whatever purpose the sceptre picked me to fulfil as its wielder."

Otherwise, I'd be stuck with it for another year. The horror. Pity I still didn't know *what*, exactly, the sceptre wanted me to do. Being a giant magical stick, it couldn't talk.

"You mean… what you saw in the Seeing Stone."

I inclined my head. The Seeing Stone—a kind of all-purpose crystal ball that didn't require one to be a Seer to glimpse the future inside it—had shown me that I'd have to use the sceptre against some unnamed threat. Given that I was the family outcast with a less-than-stellar record when it came to meeting the coven's standards, the fact that the sceptre believed I was the person best suited to meet the challenge was more worrying than flattering.

"The Seeing Stone can't actually see the future, can it?" he went on. "You don't know for sure that it'll happen that way."

"No, but the Stone has a sense of how events will progress if certain choices are made," I said, "which I realise is pretty vague, but seeing the future is complicated. It's why Seers tend to couch their predictions in confusing explanations so nobody will ask too many questions."

"I get it," he said. "You saw one possible path, which might not end up coming true if you or someone else makes a deci-sion that sends the future in a different direction."

"Yeah, there's a reason these people don't sell lottery tick-ets." Though it was beyond me to figure out how the sceptre had "known" the future the Seeing Stone had predicted. "Honestly, even most Head Witches don't know the mechanics of how the sceptres and Seeing Stones work."

The sceptre, I knew, had been created by some of the first covens a thousand years or so back, but the actual history behind the title wasn't something I'd studied in-depth. I'd checked out a few texts from a magical library a few weeks ago to see what paths a Head Witch could take, but I hadn't thought to look up where the sceptres had originated.

"Who *did* make the sceptres?" Harvey asked. "Expert wand-makers? I expect their skills are in high demand."

"Even wand-makers are rare." Very few covens had the gift of creating magical instruments, but sceptres were like a regular wand amplified by a thousand, and each of them was assigned to a single Head Witch. As far as I knew, there hadn't been any new ones created in a long while. "I don't know who made them. Not sure even Mum does."

"You'd think this kind of thing would be on record."

"You haven't seen the coven's filing cabinets. I can't even find last *week's* records in there."

The covens insisted on keeping all their records on paper instead of storing them digitally, with the result that a lot of decisions were made according to tradition without anyone knowing the original reason said tradition had formed.

One such example was the notion that each sceptre had to pick its wielder every Samhain and it could only be held by a limited selection of magical families with nobody new being allowed a look-in. I'd caused enough of a scandal by being chosen, and I *did* belong to the Wildwood Coven's founding family. But everyone had honoured the sceptre's choice regardless of their personal feelings on my capability to handle the role.

"Still," Harvey said. "Didn't we learn about the founding covens at school?"

"I must have slept through that lesson."

Since my family had held the sceptre for nearly a century, one would think they'd have some idea, but Grandma had been of no use whatsoever in passing on helpful knowledge. It'd taken long enough to convince her to start teaching me how to use the sceptre to cast spells, and she'd only agreed to that after I'd dodged several assassination attempts.

"Me too," Harvey said mildly. "I was more likely to be napping in class or daydreaming about flying than taking notes."

"At least your daydreaming became a career." I'd been inattentive at best through school, but it would have been impossible to live up to my overachieving brother even if I'd been top of the class. "My daydreams were mostly about becoming a Pokémon trainer."

He grinned. "You got Tansy. She's almost the same thing."

"I don't want to get stuck inside a Pokéball," Tansy objected from under the table, where she was eating any stray crumbs that we dropped on the floor.

"He was joking," I told my familiar. "Don't worry. You're cuter."

"Obviously." She hopped onto the table and preened, waving her fluffy tail. "I haven't forgotten you almost named me 'Eevee.'"

"My mother put a stop to that one," I explained for Harvey's benefit. "She said I had to choose a more sensible name."

As a kid, I hadn't had the clout to argue. While I'd caved in on that particular issue, I'd never intended to let my family have control over my destiny. Before I became Head Witch, my plan had been to save enough money for a nice camera to build my photography hobby. Then my brother had bribed me into staying in town by buying me said camera. That didn't mean I'd forgotten my eventual plan. Date nights aside, I would never be free to choose my own fate as long as I stayed in Wildwood Heath.

"When did you two meet?" Harvey asked. "I have a hard time imagining Tansy sitting patiently at the familiar shop waiting to be chosen."

"She wasn't," I said. "My mother asked my brother and me what kind of familiars we wanted and then used her connections to find the most likely candidates. I always wanted a red squirrel, and she pulled strings to get one from somewhere up north."

"Nice of her."

"I guess it was." I watched Tansy gambol around the table, a tightening sensation in my chest.

I'd been lucky as a kid—spoiled, even—but it had all been contingent upon my following the family's rules and being what they expected me to be. I wished I could have the perks of staying in town without the downsides, but my family was more likely to relocate to Mars than give me leeway to choose my own path. "I didn't expect her to follow through, but I remember the day I woke up and went downstairs to find this adorable ball of red fluff sitting on the kitchen table. I fell in love with Tansy right away."

"And I fell in love with you when you rescued me from your brother," Tansy remarked. "He was lecturing me on the family's rules."

"Typical of him." I fished in my bag for my camera. "Luckily, they couldn't control the personality of the familiar they picked for me."

"Normal familiars are boring." Tansy struck a pose when she saw the camera, and I snapped a few photos of her.

"Those are great," Harvey said, peering over my shoulder at the preview on my camera screen. "Are you going to do anything with them?"

I shrugged. "I don't really have time, but maybe I'll start an anonymous account on Witching Photography to see what people think."

My mother didn't want me drawing too much attention online—which was fair enough, given the not-infrequent attempts on my life—but a few squirrel photos posted under a false name wouldn't do any harm.

"Yeah, I guess you have a lot of other stuff going on," he said, "what with your family and your job."

I pulled a face. It was hard to forget how thoroughly the Head Witch title had permeated pretty much every aspect of my life, and I was still no closer to figuring out how the sceptre had chosen me above every other possible option. "Yeah, and on that note, I'd like to forget both of those things and enjoy the rest of our night."

"Fair enough."

He watched me snap a few more photos, while someone started playing live music in the background. A shifter band I didn't know had claimed the stage in the corner, and the twang of an acoustic guitar soothed my nerves a little.

"Got any plans for tomorrow?" he asked.

"I'm dragging Ramsey to visit Dad tomorrow morning."

"Wow, good luck," he said. "I was going to invite you to watch our practise session, but I figured you might find it a little boring. Though I might be free afterwards if you want to drop by in the evening."

"I promised Rowan I'd play video games with her..." Though come to think of it, I'd never actually been to his house, which might explain why we hadn't taken our relationship any further than a few kisses. The idea of inviting him to stay in my family's old house was out of the question, so my only option was to wait for him to ask me first. "She won't mind if I cancel."

"Nah, it's fine," he said. "The team will want to hang out at the pub in the evening, and you should make the most of your day off."

"I enjoy spending time with you as well." I just wished I had more of it, and I hoped he knew I was never inviting him into my mother's home.

Especially if Grandma did figure out how to get into the house. After the close call we'd had earlier, I wasn't taking any chances.

I hadn't planned to end up living in my family home again in my mid-twenties, but then again, I hadn't planned to be Head Witch either. If you asked me, I'd have made a better Pokémon trainer instead.

2

The first thing I did when I woke up the following morning was to make sure Grandma's ghost hadn't come into the house before I took a shower. Luckily, she seemed to have given up the adventuring for now, and there was no sign of her hovering outside the house when I came downstairs.

Our family's chef, Kimberly, had left the usual spread on the breakfast table, where Ramsey sat with his blond head bowed over a copy of the local newspaper. His hedgehog familiar, Prickles, managed to look dignified even while sitting on the table and lapping from a saucer of milk. As I parked myself at the table, I glimpsed Tansy in the back garden, chasing the local pigeons away from the bird feeder in a considerably less dignified manner.

"Hey, Ramsey." I grabbed a plate. "Where's Mum?"

He lifted his head from the paper. "At the office."

"Of course she is." I gave an eye roll. "There's absolutely nothing urgent going on, so why's she there? Unless she's setting out firm boundaries to keep Grandma out of the house?"

He sipped from a mug of coffee. "Grandma came into the house?"

"No, but it was a close call." I shuddered. "She got as far as the front garden, but I'm going to put sage around my room if she gets any closer. I don't need her lecturing me out of office hours as well as at work."

"It *is* her house, technically." He folded the newspaper neatly and laid it on the table. "Frankly, I'm surprised this didn't happen sooner."

"Ghosts aren't supposed to be able to wander around at will." I stacked some toast on my plate and began ladling jam onto it. "There's a reason most of them don't stick around."

"Grandma isn't most people."

"You've got that right." I bit into my toast as he rose to his feet. "Where are you going?"

"Work."

"I thought you had the day off."

"I did, but someone called in sick, so I'm going into the office."

I should have guessed from his smart suit, but he dressed casually so rarely that I hadn't thought anything of it. Scowling, I returned my attention to my plate.

"What's the problem, Robin?" he asked. "I could hardly ask the others to work on a weekend. I don't mind going into the office."

That makes one of us. It was a little unfair that he'd got the entirety of the family's workaholic tendencies and I'd inherited none. If you asked me, it would solve a lot of our problems if things had been a little more evenly split.

"I thought," I said around a mouthful of toast, "you were going to come with me to see Dad."

He paused in his path to the door. "I don't remember agreeing to that."

"You did, the other night." I swallowed my mouthful. "When we were watching *Die Hard*."

"We didn't set a specific date."

"We said 'the weekend'," I corrected. "You also said you had today off."

He gave the faintest sigh, as if I'd deeply annoyed him by suggesting he was anything less than infallible. "I'll come another time."

"Funny how you never skip out on any other appointments."

"I have a busy job, Robin," he said. "So do you, if you've forgotten."

That was uncalled for. "Yes, but I also have a family outside of the coven who has an equal right to my time. If you want to spend the sunny weather sitting behind the desk with only Prickles for company, though, be my guest."

His hedgehog familiar gave me a haughty look in response and hopped off the table to join Ramsey. While I'd long accepted that I would be wasting my time trying to convince him to get a life, I thought we'd made *some* progress. At least my brother was no longer refusing to acknowledge our father's existence, but he'd never met Dad's new partner nor her adorable kids, and this was the latest in a series of excuses he'd trotted out. His loss, I always said, but it was infuriating all the same.

Seeing Dad always cheered me up, though, so I finished breakfast and went into the back garden to fetch Tansy. A gate at the rear led directly to the woodland path that wove deep into the Wildwood and was the quickest route to my dad's cottage. He and Jessica lived in the part of town that was mostly inhabited by shifters who wanted the privacy of the woods to shift and the empty space to run around in their animal forms without encountering any unwitting humans. As a bonus, the surroundings were positively picturesque, enough to make me wish I'd brought my camera to snag some pictures of the towering oaks shading the small cottage.

When I knocked, Dad answered the door with his customary smile. Short and chubby with thinning hair, he looked positively ordinary compared to my other family members, which was a welcome sight after a week of dealing with snooty coven members. He wrapped me in a hug and waved at Tansy, who flicked her tail in greeting from her perch on a tree branch.

"Jessica's out for a run in the woods with the boys," Dad said, leading me into the hallway. "I've no chance of keeping up with three shifters, so I'm doing things around the house."

"You didn't want to go outside?" I gestured to the window in the living room. "It's England's one sunny day of the year."

"We can sit in the garden," he suggested. "I'd be left in the dust if I tried to join the others. Besides, I wanted to see you."

"I wouldn't be able to keep up with them either."

I'd recently taken up jogging in the woods a few times a week just to get some exercise when I wasn't in the office, but I liked to go at my own pace. That tendency was a point of contention between me and my other family members, who couldn't fathom doing anything for fun rather than competitively. No wonder Dad and I got along so much better.

We pulled a couple of deck chairs out to the garden and caught up on the past week, while Tansy amused herself climbing trees and chasing off any local grey squirrels who encroached on her territory.

"I tried to convince Ramsey to come, but he's at work," I told Dad. "Said someone took the day off so he had to step in."

"I thought so," Dad said. "I don't mind. He's always welcome here."

"I keep telling him that." I sighed. "I really thought I had him this time, but it's like he can't fathom *making* time for other people the way he does for his work. He seems to think the office will implode if he isn't there."

"Takes after your mother."

"Unfortunately."

Dad didn't hold anything against Mum for the way things had ended between them, and if anything, he'd taken the fallout better than I had. Being ordinary was the only crime he'd committed in the eyes of the press and other admirers of my family, who viewed him as not worthy of being involved with the coven. It forever infuriated me that they couldn't see past the family name to realise that anyone else had value.

Dad, ever the pragmatist, just shrugged. "As long as he's happy."

"Happy to miss out on the nice weather."

I shaded my eyes from a sunbeam as Tansy scampered above us and rattled the tree branches. "I should have brought my camera."

"You're managing to find time to take photos?"

"Not as much as I'd like." I hadn't even explored most of the camera's features, though Tansy was more than happy to model for me. "Mostly I'm trying to figure out how to share them online without my mother griping at me for painting a target on my head."

"Can't you use a fake name?"

"Yeah, but it wouldn't take much for someone to guess my location," I explained. "That's what Mum said anyway."

The magical world consisted of insular small communities scattered across the UK, but with the Wizarding Web connecting everyone online, it was easier to find someone than it used to be. Add in my family's highly public nature, and I'd had a hard time keeping a low profile even when I'd been living away from them. Now that there were people legitimately trying to assassinate me, odds were I'd have to shake off the Head Witch title before I could pursue my photography hobby in any serious capacity.

"I'm sure it'd be fine if you were careful," he said. "It's not like you'd be posting photos of your mother's house, is it?"

"No, but you know what she's like."

Dad had experienced her intensity first-hand in the years they'd been married, and it was no wonder he'd retreated to the middle of the woods upon being set free.

To be fair, the pair of them had been civil to one another the last time they'd talked face to face, but Dad was easy-going by nature, and my mother prized keeping up appearances and self-control. The latter, I wouldn't mind having inherited, but she and my brother could keep the workaholism. I was content to sit here and enjoy the sunshine and the birdsong… Wait. Was that screaming I heard?

I sat upright, relaxing a little when I recognised the squealing as belonging to a couple of excitable children. "They're back already?"

"Looks that way." Dad climbed to his feet and stood on tiptoe to see over the fence. "Ah—Jessica?"

The gate clicked open and two entirely nude kids came running into the garden. Shifters usually shed their clothes when they changed into their animal forms, and while they didn't have the same hang-ups about nudity as non-shifters did, it was usually something one wanted to be forewarned about when walking in the woods.

Jessica peered around the fence—unlike the kids, she'd wrapped a robe around herself—and called to them. "Spike, Jake, go back in the house, okay?"

Her sweaty face wasn't that strange for a shifter who'd just come back from a run, but the tension in her voice and her haunted expression drew me to my feet. "What happened?"

"We found a body in the woods," piped up one of the small children.

"A body?" Dad stared at him then at Jessica. "Please tell me you're playing a game."

"I wish we were." Jessica entered the garden, tying the robe around her waist. "Boys, go inside and clean yourselves up."

The boys obeyed, chattering to one another. They didn't appear overly shaken up by the experience, but they weren't old enough to know the significance of what the words meant. A body in the woods… The last time one of those had shown up, it had ended in an attempt on my life.

"A body?" Dad repeated. "Whose?"

"I don't know," said Jessica. "A shifter, I think, but not someone I recognised."

The colour drained from Dad's face. "Are the boys all right?"

From the shrieks inside the house, the two of them had already started play fighting again, which I assumed meant they were just fine.

Jessica approached the door. "I shooed them away from the body when I realised what it was, but they already saw."

"I'll call the police," I offered. "Ah—I'd have to give them directions, though. How far away is it?"

"It'd be easier if I led them there myself," Jessica said, glancing at the house. "But the boys…"

"I'll watch them," Dad said. "But—if there's something dangerous out there, I don't want you going out alone."

"I'll go with her." I wished I hadn't left my sceptre behind. If there was a magical monster on the loose, the sceptre wouldn't necessarily deter it, but at least I'd feel a little more secure.

"Ask your brother instead," he said. "He'll send in a team, I expect."

"Yes, but someone needs to show them where to go, don't they?" I pointed out. "I'd grab my sceptre from home, but then I'd get lassoed into a conversation with my mother."

Dad's mouth turned down at the corners. "If you're sure, but please don't put yourself in danger."

"I'll be fine."

If we ran into anything nasty, I had my wand, and Jessica could shift into a wolf. If you asked me, the latter stood more chance of intimidating a wild animal than my sceptre did.

I grabbed my phone and called my brother's number. As I'd expected, he answered right away.

"Hey, Ramsey," I said, before he could get out a word. "Sorry to drag you out of work, but there's a dead body in the forest."

A brief pause, in which I heard a faint sigh. "Why is it always you, Robin?"

"Technically it wasn't me this time. Jessica found the body. If you send in a team, we can show you where it is."

"No, you most certainly won't," he said. "You stay put, and I'll come myself."

He ended the call, and I shook my head at the phone. "Okay, then."

"He wants us to stay here?" Jessica surmised.

"You don't have to listen to him." I paced towards the gate. "Neither do I, for that matter. He can catch us up."

"Are you sure?" She gave Dad a worried look and then faced the trees overlooking the fence. "Where's your familiar?"

"She won't be far away. I can ask her to help keep the boys entertained while we're gone."

I ducked out of the gate and whistled, calling Tansy to come scampering down the nearest tree trunk.

"I heard," Tansy told me. "Another body showed up in the woods?"

"Yeah," I said. "Ramsey is on this way, but Jessica could use a hand keeping the boys distracted. Can you do that?"

"My pleasure." She scurried across the fence.

Jessica and Dad exchanged a few quiet words, then Jessica strode across the garden while Dad reluctantly backed into the house.

"We'll be right back," Jessica called to the boys. "Behave for your dad, won't you?"

I let her lead the way since I wasn't familiar with the deeper part of the woods. Most of the paths weren't made for humans, as they'd been created by shifters in werewolf form barging through the undergrowth. As a result, I had to frequently climb over bushes and use my wand to disperse thick greenery as I followed Jessica deeper into the Wildwood.

While I knew intellectually that we weren't far from civilisation even amid the maze of thick oak trees, the quietness of the forest gained an ominous hint, especially knowing what lay ahead. I didn't blame Jessica for being on edge. Every few steps, she raised her head and sniffed at the air. Shifters had powerful senses, so she would know if there was anyone here who shouldn't be. The canopy was thick enough to cut out most of the sunlight, with the result that I nearly walked straight past the body.

The man—boy, really—looked as if he was sleeping. He was barely out of his teens, gangly and awkward with a nest of shaggy brown hair. He was also naked, having recently shifted from animal to human, which made it immediately obvious that he didn't have a scratch on him.

"Erm… are you sure he's dead?"

I turned to Jessica, who sniffed the air again.

"I can smell it," she said. "I don't know how he died, though."

"The police should be able to figure it out."

At least he didn't appear to have been attacked by a monster, which had been the fate of the last person to turn up dead in the forest. The shifters had taken a fair bit of flack for that, as Tiffany Henbane had tried to deflect blame from her coven onto the local werewolves instead.

"What kind of shifter is he, do you know?" I asked.

"A badger shifter, from his scent."

By the looks of things, he hadn't fought back against his attacker, though badgers could be vicious when they wanted to be. In fact, he appeared to have been taken by surprise.

"I wonder why he was so deep in the woods?"

Most people had more sense than to walk off the trails in the Wildwood alone, but given his age, he might have been lacking in that department. I scanned the nearby bushes in search of clues, and my gaze landed on a shoe sticking out of the undergrowth. Following that direction, I saw more clothes strewn around the area as well an abandoned rucksack.

Jessica sucked in a breath. "I think he was camping."

I followed her gaze and saw a collapsed tent across the entrance to a clearing, nestled between tall trees. "Then he wasn't alone."

I left the path and trekked into the clearing, where several other tents lay, along with more abandoned clothes and backpacks. *Who'd go camping in the Wildwood?* A bunch of reckless teens, evidently, but if there'd been more than one badger shifter here, where were the others?

"There were three… maybe four of them." Jessica reached the middle of the clearing, nostrils flaring as her werewolf senses went into overdrive. "Four in total. They were here recently too."

"Something attacked them."

The frantic footprints in the churned-up mud made it clear that they'd been chased off, but by what, or whom? A chill ran down my spine at the memory of the deadly beast that had attacked a couple of the visiting Head Witches a few weeks ago, summoned by Tiffany Henbane. Was she up to her old tricks again, even from behind bars? *The victim didn't have a mark on him, though...*

"I can't smell their attacker." Jessica stiffened. "Someone else is coming, though."

"Robin," said a breathless voice.

I spun around as my brother came running into view at surprising speed for someone who spent the majority of his time hunched over a desk.

"Robin—get away from there."

"Relax, there's nobody here," I told him. "Jessica would have smelled them."

"I thought I told you to stay away from the body." He reached the clearing, his gaze roving around the abandoned tents before fixating on the unfortunate shifter's corpse.

"How'd *you* find us?" I asked.

"Your familiar." He indicated Tansy, who came bounding out of the undergrowth and wagged her tail at me.

"You left me behind," Tansy accused me.

"I thought you *wanted* to help entertain the kids," I protested. "I didn't think you'd want to see a dead body either."

"You shouldn't be here," Ramsey repeated. "Neither of you should."

He didn't look directly at Jessica, and I wondered if he even recognised her as Dad's new partner. They'd never been formally introduced, though not for lack of effort on Dad's part—or mine.

Jessica herself didn't look surprised at Ramsey's reaction. "I'm sorry. I'll go..."

"You don't have to," I said.

To Ramsey, I added, "The other campers might be around

somewhere. Jessica sniffed out four in total, and they haven't gone far from here."

"I have shifters on my team," Ramsey said. "This is a matter for the police to deal with."

"Ramsey." How many times did we have to have the same argument? "They're right here in the forest, unlike your team. Their attacker might be here too."

"That's more reason for you to leave," he said. "You don't even have your sceptre with you."

"No, because it's my day off." I should have known that decision would come back to bite me, but how was I supposed to know *another* body would show up in the woods? "You didn't bring backup either. Did you run here alone?"

"What do you think?" He strode into the clearing. "I might remind you that you're even less entitled to be here if you aren't acting in the capacity of Head Witch."

"Pedant." I moved over to Jessica. "Ignore him. Which direction do the other scents lead to?"

She lifted her head. "They're tangled together, so it's hard to tell. I think this way…"

She crossed the clearing, passing the ruined tents, while Ramsey kept up a stream of objections in the background. I tuned him out and followed Jessica through the under-growth, Tansy scampering onto my shoulder to avoid getting tangled in the bushes.

"The shifters must be locals, right?" Tansy said into my ear. "Nobody else knows the way around."

"This way," Jessica directed me.

Jessica wove through the trees, while my brother reluc-tantly followed our path. When she came to a sudden halt, Tansy let out an exclamation and leapt off my shoulder onto a low-hanging tree branch.

"Whoa." I took a step back as three badgers ran out of the

bushes and then vanished into the undergrowth almost as quickly as they'd appeared.

While I was trying to pinpoint where they'd run to, Ramsey came dashing up to us with his wand in his hand.

"What the—?" Ramsey said.

"Look at that." I indicated the nearest badger's tail, which stuck out from under a bush. "I think we found your missing campers. You're welcome."

Ramsey lowered his wand. "Police here. Come out of those bushes and turn into your human forms to be questioned."

3

The three badgers responded to Ramsey's command by emerging from the bushes for a second time and shifting into humans one by one. All of them were male and around eighteen, like the unfortunate guy we'd found dead in the bushes. They were also naked, and there was a great deal of awkward scrambling to grab clothes from the mess strewn around the clearing while Ramsey fired questions at them.

"What happened to your friend?" he called out.

"Don't know," returned one of the shifters, holding up a shoe. "Is this your shoe, Ralph?"

"No, it's Phil's." Ralph gestured at the body of their unlucky friend with a trembling hand. "What... what happened to him?"

"He's dead!" The third shifter, having failed to notice the obvious until this moment, let out a wail of despair and then shifted into a badger again.

As the badger landed on all fours, I raised a brow at Ramsey. "Are you sure you don't want to wait for the rest of your team before you start the questioning?"

Ramsey ignored me and addressed the shifters, two of whom were fully dressed while the badger-shaped one had buried himself underneath a discarded jacket. "Did any of you see what happened to your friend?"

"No, it was dark," said Ralph, who was taller and ganglier than the other shifters and had an unfortunate haircut that looked as if he'd cut it himself with a pair of nail clippers.

"At noon?" asked Ramsey. "How long have you been hiding in the bushes?"

"Don't know," said Ralph's friend, whose acne-ridden brow was furrowed in confusion. "It was dark."

"What were you doing in the forest to begin with?" Ramsey gestured to the clearing. "You must have known the risks of camping here."

Ralph winced. "We live near the forest. I didn't think it was illegal to go camping."

"It's not, but something chased you, didn't it?" I gestured at the clearing. "Didn't you see what it was?"

"No." Ralph eyed the third shifter, who was still hiding underneath a coat in the form of a badger. "It went dark, and then I panicked and shifted. I think the others did too."

"You didn't see what happened to your friend?" I asked.

The guy hadn't a scratch on him. The chaos in the clearing might have been caused by four panicking badger shifters, but their friend couldn't have dropped dead without any cause.

"Do you think a… a witch or wizard attacked you?" I could think of a few spells that could cause it to go pitch-black during the day, but why would a witch or wizard randomly attack a group of camping badger shifters?

"I don't think so," said Ralph. "I did hear a noise that didn't sound like a badger. It was a bit like… like snarling or growling."

"You were here in the clearing at the time?" Ramsey asked. "All of you? What time was this?"

"We slept in late," said Ralph. "We'd just come out of our tents when everything went dark."

Slept in? That was plausible, given their ages, but I found it hard to believe that a section of the forest had gone completely pitch-black in the middle of the day without anyone else in the region noticing.

"Did you see anyone else nearby?" I asked.

"No." The acne-ridden shifter's eyes widened suddenly. "Wait, aren't you the Head Witch?"

Finally, the penny dropped.

"Yes. My dad's partner was jogging in the woods when she found your friend's body, and she didn't mention it being any darker than normal."

"It wasn't," mumbled Ralph. "I mean, not for long. We panicked and stayed hidden in case the darkness came back."

"I see," Ramsey said. "All three of you will come to the police station with me. Robin, you go home—and that *is* an order. Is that clear?"

"Crystal."

I wanted to hear what the campers had to say for themselves, but I had an inkling I'd be excluded from sitting in on the questioning. As my brother insisted upon reminding me on a regular basis, helping the police wasn't my job. Yes, I'd been an asset on more than one occasion, but those incidents had involved my position as Head Witch, so he'd been forced to make an exception.

Then again, for all I knew, this incident might end up linking to the previous attempts on my life as well. It wasn't the first time a monster had appeared in the woods, and the last incident had been a result of Tiffany's attempt to both undermine the Wildwood Coven and destroy our credibility in the eyes of the press—by killing off the other Head

Witches. Tiffany was currently in jail, but if someone had picked up where she'd left off, it was very much my business.

While the two guys attempted to coax their friend to shift into a human again, I moved to my brother's side. "Are you sure you don't want my help with this? I'm not exactly unfamiliar with mysterious monsters attacking people in the woods."

"That was different," he said. "This doesn't sound like a monster. It sounds like several friends got confused and scared one another."

"And one of them dropped dead without so much as a scratch on him?"

Instead of answering, Ramsey turned towards the path, where the sound of several pairs of feet tramping through the undergrowth announced the arrival of the other officers. "The rest of my team's here. If you go home, I'll let you know how the questioning goes when I'm done."

"I'll hold you to that."

I approached Jessica, who watched the advancing officers warily.

"Want to head back?" I asked.

She gave a nod. "Your familiar's up there somewhere."

I lifted my gaze to the trees. "She might have gone back to the cottage."

The last incident in the woods had freaked her out, so I didn't blame Tansy for running off. Yet this situation both echoed and diverged from the last one, which bugged me in ways that I couldn't quite put my finger on. *What spell causes total darkness? More to the point, why would someone use it against a bunch of harmless camping teenagers?*

"Is it normal for teenage shifters to go camping in the woods?" I asked Jessica as we walked back, somewhat relieved to leave the badger shifters behind.

"It's not unheard of," she replied. "I don't know what they

meant about it being dark, though. Everything looked completely normal when the boys and I were in the woods."

"It must have been a spell. If they're telling the truth, that is."

Verifying the shifters' stories was Ramsey's job, of course, but I wished he'd been more open to accepting my help.

"I'm sorry my brother was so, er, blunt. I kept telling him that he should come and visit so you didn't have to be introduced while he was in work mode, which was bound to happen eventually."

Jessica winced. "You don't think *you* might have been the target of whatever attacked those shifters, do you?"

"I don't know that for sure." I'd forgotten not everyone would understand my casual attitude towards the recent attempts on my life, but it was that or run around screaming. "Don't worry. I just have a knack for running into trouble, that's all."

"I know I shouldn't have taken the boys that deep in the woods." She slowed as we reached the cottage, where Jake and Spike came running out of the garden to greet her.

Dad waited for me by the front door. "Does your brother have the situation handled?"

"He thinks he does."

In fairness, there wasn't much Ramsey could do, given that the forest was a veritable maze and there'd been no obvious clues pointing to the killer's identity. It had hardly looked like a murder at all.

"I should give you guys some peace," I said.

"The kids seem to be doing fine," Dad replied. "Thanks to your familiar."

On cue, Tansy came scurrying across the fence and hopped into her favourite position on my shoulder.

"I wondered where you got to." I stroked Tansy from her head to her fluffy tail.

"I don't like badger shifters," Tansy said in my ear. "They smell."

"Well, they're in my brother's hands now." For Dad's benefit, I added, "They seem to think someone cast a spell on their campsite to make it go pitch-black and then caused one of them to drop dead. Their story is full of more holes than a pair of my old socks."

"I'm sure Ramsey will straighten them out," Dad said. "You'll be careful, won't you?"

"As much as I ever am." While that might not be a reassurance, I made a point of being honest with Dad. "I'll let you know if my brother finds anything out. He told me he'd give me an update if I was sensible and went home."

Not that the idea of enduring a lecture from my mother was appealing. She'd find a way to twist the situation into being my fault, and it was too early in the day to resign myself to being stuck in Mum's house waiting for Grandma's next inevitable excursion.

"*Are* you going to be sensible and go home?" Tansy asked as we left Dad's cottage behind.

"Nope," I replied. "I'm going to see Rowan. Ramsey can hardly lecture me for that. It's not like I'll be anywhere near the forest."

Midday on Saturday was the cafe's busiest time, but Rowan was always up for a chat. If I had to break the news of yet another murder in the woods, she'd take it much better than Mum would.

Tansy lifted her head. "Did your brother hire some new officers?"

"No, I don't think so." I kept walking. "Why?"

"I smell someone… unfamiliar." She wrapped her tail around the back of my neck. "I don't like them."

"What do you mean, you don't like them? You can't see them."

Baffled, I kept walking until the murmur of voices caught my ear from somewhere to the east, on the path that led from Dad's cottage back to the witches' part of town.

As we drew closer, my ears picked out two voices: one male and one female. They sounded like they were arguing, and I strained my ears, trying to hear what the voices were saying.

"I told you to bring a map," said the male voice. "Now we're lost."

"We aren't lost," the woman retaliated. "There's a street over there, see? And houses."

"Congratulations on passing your eye test," drawled the male voice. "Also, did it occur to you that we might be trespassing?"

"What makes you say that?"

"This looks too orderly to be a nature trail."

"Tansy," I whispered to my familiar, "can you get closer and tell me what they look like?"

"They?" She reared upright on my shoulder, her body tensed. "There's only one person."

"I heard two."

I watched Tansy jump to the nearest low-hanging branch, and then I approached the pair, my gaze picking out the woman first. She stood with her back to me, and I assumed she was a witch from the way she'd failed to notice her proximity to the shifters' territory. Her long dark hair and casual jeans and T-shirt didn't make her look particularly threatening. She wasn't local, but I couldn't tell what had got Tansy so agitated.

As I stepped onto the path, the woman spun around and pulled a wand out of her sleeve. "Whoa. Sorry, you startled me."

"Who are you?" Where was her companion? Unless she was an exceptionally good voice actress, there'd been someone else here too. A familiar, perhaps? "I'm Robin. You're not local, are you?"

"I'm Maura," she answered. "I'm also lost. Is this the Wildwood?"

"Yes, it is."

Weird. The town wasn't signposted, but our few tourists didn't make a habit of arriving on foot.

"You didn't walk all the way through the woods, did you?" I asked.

"Not exactly."

Her gaze flickered to the bushes, and her companion slid into view. Like her, he was pale and dark-haired, with enough of a resemblance to her that made me guess they were siblings. There was just one major difference: the man was dead, while the woman was very much alive.

"You were talking to a ghost."

I stared at the man—or boy, really—and he gave me a cheeky grin in return.

"That," said Maura, "is my brother, Mart. I didn't know you could see ghosts."

"It's not that uncommon around here." I frowned. "Aren't ghosts supposed to be tied to a single location?"

"Most are, but there are a few exceptions."

Like my grandmother. What were the odds of running into another?

"I'm Maura's essential partner in crime," Mart announced. "This place is very *green*, isn't it?"

"Where'd you come from?" I asked.

"Hawkwood Hollow," Maura answered. "You probably haven't heard of it. It's a tiny village in the northwest of England."

I didn't know it, though that might be because I had trouble remembering place names at the best of times. "What brings you here?"

"A ghost," she said. "A friend of ours is a ghost blogger. We're scouting for new filming locations."

"We don't have any haunted houses. We're not that kind of town."

In fact, the most notable ghost in town was my grandmother, and over my own dead body was I introducing the two of them to one another. Ghost or no ghost, Mum would send our visitors packing the instant she found out they wanted to use the town as a filming location. We didn't need any more unnecessary publicity... but the timing of her arrival drew my suspicion for another reason entirely.

"I figured," she said. "Like I said, I'm lost. There aren't maps of the forest, are there?"

"No, which is why I find it hard to believe you got through there without help."

A ghost for a companion would have been an asset, given that he could float straight through the trees until he found civilisation, but she certainly didn't look as if she'd been walking in the forest for days. An hour or two, if that. "You're a witch, right?"

"Yes, and I have a good sense of direction."

Hmm. "It's not the directions that are the issue. The woods are full of dangers, as any local would tell you."

"I don't scare easily either." She nodded to Mart. "Being around ghosts tends to cure you of that."

She wasn't an ordinary witch, I was sure, but she hadn't mentioned my Head Witch title. If she didn't know me, she was unlikely to be a potential assassin or rival to my position, but I didn't believe that she'd come here by accident either.

All right. I'd call her bluff. "I'm Robin Wildwood. My coven owns this forest, along with the town of Wildwood Heath."

Her eyes widened. "Ah. I didn't know I was that close to a coven's territory."

"I take it you don't belong to one yourself?"

"No," she said. "Covens and I don't tend to see eye to eye."

I know the feeling. I stamped down the urge to say so aloud and instead asked, "Why are you really here?"

"I told you, I'm chasing a ghost," she replied. "I didn't know there was a town in the middle of the woods, but if you're sure there aren't any ghosts in the area, we'll leave. Right, Mart?"

"Really?" His face fell. "Can't we at least look around? This place looks like fun."

"Fun?" Every word they said made it seem less and less likely that they'd attacked those campers, but my suspicions remained intact. "I don't think you should leave. In fact, you should meet my brother. He's the head of the local police."

Maura's brows shot up. "Because we're trespassing?"

"No. Right before we saw you, a body showed up in the woods."

Maura followed my gaze as I pointed in the direction of where we'd found the body.

"Seriously?"

"Yes, and I don't think the rest of my coven would be pleased if I let a potential suspect walk away."

Maura vanished. One moment she stood in front of me, and the next it was as if the ground had swallowed her up. As I blinked, her brother gave me an apologetic look.

"Gotta run. See you around," he said.

With a brief salute, he disappeared too. Vanishing into thin air made more sense for a ghost than a human, but she hadn't even waved her wand.

"How did she move so fast?"

"I don't know." Tansy dropped from the tree branch onto my shoulder. "It looked as if she… she walked through her own shadow."

My gaze snapped downward. Was it my imagination, or

did the shadows on the forest floor appear a little thicker than before? I recalled the shifters' story of total darkness descending over their camp, and a shiver raced down my spine. "All right, she's definitely a suspect."

The ghost who accompanied her was proof enough that she had abilities that weren't the domain of us mere mortals, though I didn't know what Ramsey would make of her. Assuming I managed to find her again. I walked to the spot where Maura had vanished, where not a single trace of her was left but a faint chill lingered in the air.

"I knew she smelled weird." Tansy's fur stood on end and her body trembled. "Creepy."

"Creepy? Like… like whatever attacked those guys?"

"Maybe."

"Right." I drew upright. "I'm going to get my sceptre, and then I'll go and tell my brother."

4

Luckily, Mum wasn't home from the office yet, so I was able to slip upstairs to my room and snag my sceptre without having to break the news of the shifter's death. With my sceptre in hand, I left the house again and followed the main street to the centre of Wildwood Heath.

Tansy scurried at my side, having seemingly recovered from her scare in the forest. We weren't far from the café where Rowan worked, but I figured that she'd be slammed with customers at this time of day, so I opted to head for the police station first.

The automatic doors slid open, and I entered, waving at the receptionist, Julian. A weasel shifter with a complex for cleanliness, he was currently on his knees with a dustpan and brush cleaning up a trail of mud and leaves that I assumed the campers had left behind them. Julian always wore a disgruntled expression when he saw me, though the sight of the sceptre in my hand quashed any protests he might have voiced.

Ramsey, who was in the process of herding the three

campers into the waiting room, closed the door on them and strode over to me. "Robin, I told you to go home."

"I found a suspect in the woods," I told him. "Not a local. She claimed to be chasing a ghost, but she gave me the slip before I could bring her here."

His jaw tightened. "How can you have already run into a suspect when I only left you a few minutes ago?"

"I have a knack." I gestured to my familiar, who scurried up my arm and sat on my shoulder. "Actually, it was Tansy who spotted her. The woman wasn't local and claimed that she didn't know anyone lived here in the middle of the woods, but she clearly didn't walk here on foot, either."

"How'd you lose her?" He eyed my sceptre. "You didn't have that with you."

"It wouldn't have made a difference if I did," I said defensively. "Tansy said it looked like she walked into her own shadow and disappeared."

"Walked into her own shadow." Scepticism dripped from his voice. "Are you sure she didn't just use a transportation spell?"

"She did have her wand in her hand," I acknowledged, "but I didn't see her use it. Oh, and she had the ghost of her twin brother with her too."

"That's not possible," he said. "Ghosts can't move around."

"Grandma did it yesterday, remember?" He was just arguing for the sake of it, I was sure. "She said she stumbled upon the town by accident, but I don't think that's very likely, do you?"

He sighed. "Robin, I'm going to question the campers, but you can tell me more about the suspect afterwards. And her… ghost."

"I'll be waiting in the café." I stepped away from Julian, who was trying to brush the floor near my feet, and left the police station for Were's My Coffee?

The werewolf-run café had become my cousin Rowan's new home after she'd finally broken free from her scheming family members, and as I'd predicted, the café was packed. At the counter behind the dense queue of customers, my cousin shot me a smile. Rowan had dyed her hair a striking shade of bright purple since she'd moved out, and the relaxed way in which she chatted to the customers was an indication of how she'd come into her own after years of living under her unpleasant mother's thumb.

There were no tables free, but I joined the queue anyway. It looked as if the local flower club had stopped meeting here at the weekends, but their table had been taken by a boisterous group of local shifters who were engaged in a competition as to who could fit an entire croissant into their mouth without needing to shift into a wolf. Tansy eagerly positioned herself under the table to steal any crumbs people dropped, while I ordered an iced latte and a sandwich.

"How's it going, Robin?" Rowan asked as she handed over my drink. "I thought you were going to see your dad."

"Our visit got cut short when a body showed up in the woods."

Her fingers fumbled my latte, but I reached out and caught the cup before she dropped it.

"Please tell me you're joking. Whose body?"

"A group of camping badger shifters had an unpleasant surprise earlier," I answered. "Not sure how, but one of them died, and my brother is questioning the others."

Her face paled. "It can't be the Henbanes again, can it?"

"I didn't see any connection to them, but I don't believe in coincidences," I commented. "I can ask my brother if he'll have a look around their headquarters again in case he missed anything last time."

"Would he listen to you?"

"He might." I picked up my latte, noticing the customer

behind me was giving me the evil eye. "Or not. He's still at the 'stubbornly refusing to let me get involved' stage."

"Hasn't he learned that won't work?" She moved to serve the next person in line, while I spotted a free table and snagged it, sitting down to eat my sandwich while I waited for the flood of customers to die down.

When the pack of rowdy shifters finally left, Rowan came to clean their table and resume our conversation.

"Your brother's questioning the shifters, you said?" she asked. "Does he think one of them attacked their friend?"

"I don't know what he thinks." I took another sip of my iced latte. "I complicated matters by running into a potential suspect in the woods, so we'll have to see if she shows up again."

"You ran into a suspect?" She stepped around Tansy, who was hoovering up all the crumbs the shifters had dropped on the floor. "Who?"

"Not a local," I replied. "She was clearly lying when she said she stumbled upon Wildwood Heath by accident while looking for a ghost, though."

"Yeah, nobody walks into the woods without knowing where they're going."

Rowan went back to cleaning, while I checked to make sure nobody nearby was listening in. Some of the customers were regulars, including Dale Longfoot, a local shifter who'd been a murder suspect a few weeks ago. He didn't look as if he was interested in eavesdropping, so I figured I was safe to tell Rowan the truth.

When she came back to my table, I whispered, "Have you ever heard of a spell that can make someone disappear into the shadows?"

"Shadows?" she echoed. "Is that what your suspect did?"

"Yep," I said. "I don't know anything about her except her name—Maura. Oh, and she has a brother who happens to be a ghost, and she can apparently walk through the shadows to get out of unwanted conversations."

"A *ghost*?" Her brow scrunched up. "You said she was looking for a ghost here too?"

"That's what she claimed."

"Erm… Robin, you don't think she was a Reaper, do you?"

A Reaper? The thought hadn't crossed my mind, but I shook my head. "She was carrying a wand, not a scythe. Why would a Reaper come here?"

"To get rid of Grandma's ghost?"

"I wish," I said. "She learned to leave the headquarters yesterday, can you believe it?"

"Who, Grandma or the Reaper?"

"Grandma, of course," I said. "And I don't know that our suspect is a Reaper. They're supposed to be creepy hooded figures armed with giant scythes, right?"

"Yeah, but it'd explain why she has a ghost following her around," said Rowan. "Reapers have access to magic that's off limits to the rest of us mere mortals."

"Some ghosts are more stubborn than others. Look at Grandma." She did have a point, though. "Our suspect gave me the slip, so I'm unlikely to run into her again anytime soon…"

I trailed off as the door opened and Maura herself walked into the café, Mart trailing behind her. Her ghostly companion didn't attract any stares, but when Rowan followed my gaze, her jaw dropped. "Wait, is that her?"

"Yes, it is."

Upon recognising me, Maura backed straight out of the café's doors. I leapt to my feet and ran across the room, catching the door in my hand and calling to her. "Wait!"

To my great relief, she hadn't vanished into the shadows this time, though the number of bystanders around suggested she hadn't wanted to draw attention.

Tansy came scurrying out of the café and reared up onto her hind legs. "Not so fast!" she squeaked.

Maura couldn't understand Tansy, of course, but my familiar's body language spoke for itself.

"Look, I didn't want to make a scene. I only wanted a latte," Maura said.

"The lattes here are great," I acknowledged, "but they don't have special discounts for Reapers. Just saying."

"Ha." Mart snorted. "That's a good one."

"Mart." Maura shot her brother an irritated look. "Who said I was a Reaper?"

"My cousin guessed, and you aren't denying it, are you?" I narrowed my eyes. "Don't you even think about running off again."

Maura gave a sigh. "I didn't expect that I'd need to stay in town, but something came up. I'll stay out of your way while I'm here."

"You certainly won't," I said. "You were in the woods earlier when someone got attacked by a mysterious assailant, and you also claimed to be looking for a ghost."

"Someone got attacked?" She blinked at me. "You didn't mention that."

"You didn't mention you were a Reaper, so we're square."

Her mouth parted. "Whoever got attacked in the woods, that's not why I'm here."

"You're not here to banish a ghost to the afterworld?"

I didn't know a great deal about Reapers, but I was pretty sure banishing ghosts was their primary role and the reason they tended to keep to themselves. I was also under the impression that they were supposed to stay in certain regions and not wander off, though Maura must be at least half non-Reaper if she carried a wand. That would also explain why she otherwise looked human.

She shrugged one shoulder. "Depends if I find them. It's

not something that's going to affect you, though, so if you don't mind…"

"Not so fast." As the shadows thickened around her feet, I pointed the sceptre at her. The purple glow stopped her retreat, and even her ghostly brother's mouth fell open.

"You're… you're a Head Witch?" she asked.

I felt a tad insulted at how surprised she sounded, considering she didn't even know me.

"Yes, I am. I did tell you I belonged to the leading coven, didn't I?"

Maura's brother laughed. "You've really landed in it now, haven't you?"

"I'm not going to fight you," I told them both. "I just want you to answer some questions from the police."

I didn't usually like using my sceptre to intimidate people, but I couldn't even begin to imagine what kind of powers a half-Reaper might be able to unleash on me. Being able to short cut through the shadows would explain how she'd found the town without getting lost in the Wildwood, but she would have needed to know where she was going in the first place. At least that was how it worked with transportation spells: they required a clear visual of one's destination.

No, she wasn't being honest with me. What if she did know something about what had attacked those campers? I couldn't afford to let her slip away again, and despite the unwelcome stares from the public, I didn't feel too guilty about using my sceptre to herd Maura into the police station.

Julian was still trying to clean up the scattered leaves on the floor. When he saw us enter, he rose to his feet. "Who's this?"

"A suspect." I indicated the closed door to the interrogation room in the back left corner of the lobby. "Is Ramsey questioning the suspects individually?"

"Yes." Seth, a tall black man with a shaved head, answered on Julian's behalf.

I'd struck up a friendship of sorts with Seth after I'd found out he made a habit of playing Pokémon Go when he was off duty, but his expression when he saw Maura was all suspicion.

"Who's this?" Seth asked.

"Maura. She's a Reaper."

The receptionist dropped his dustpan at the word "Reaper," while Seth's eyes widened.

"Really?" Seth said.

"Yep. We'll wait for Ramsey in there."

Maura herself didn't give so much as an eye roll when Tansy and I herded her into the waiting room. My familiar planted herself in front of the door and struck a threatening stance.

"I don't suppose you're going to tell me why there's a squirrel looking at me murderously?" asked Maura.

"Tansy's my familiar." I decided not to mention my family's gift yet, in case I needed to use it to my advantage later on. "I assume you don't have one?"

"No. I have enough babysitting on my hands already." She glanced through the window in the door, which showed her ghostly brother levitating a stack of papers above the confused receptionist's desk. Raising her voice, she called to him, "Mart, cut that out."

Mart grinned and dropped the papers onto Julian's head. *I guess she doesn't need a familiar when she already has a misbehaving ghostly sibling to keep in line.*

The sound of the interrogation room door opening prompted me to peer out of the waiting area, where my own brother had emerged to find the source of the noise.

"Robin, what're you doing in there?"

"I brought your suspect," I told him. "You're welcome."

"Suspect?" Behind me, Maura stuck her head out of the waiting room, ignoring Tansy's disgruntled hissing at her feet. "Hang on a minute. I think we had a misunderstanding."

"Did you now?" Ramsey's gaze slid over to her and then back to me. "Is this the suspect you found in the woods, Robin?"

"Yes, and she's a Reaper," I added. "I thought it was wise to bring her straight here before she escaped again."

"I'm not a suspect," Maura protested. "I didn't even know anyone had been murdered until she told me."

"But you were in the woods at the same time as the attack," he said. "Which makes you a witness. You're really a Reaper?"

"Half," she said, with visible reluctance. "And that's my brother."

Ramsey did a double take at the sight of Mart, who gave him a cheery wave from behind Julian's desk. "He's a ghost…"

"Yes, he is," Maura said. "You'll have a hell of a time containing him in a cell. Fair warning."

"I don't intend to arrest either of you," Ramsey said. "I simply wanted to ask you some questions about the incident in the woods earlier today."

"I probably have more questions than you do," she said. "But fine, if you want to talk, I'll happily set the record straight."

Ramsey scowled at Mart, seemingly more annoyed at Mart's antics than at the fact that there was a Reaper in the building. Not a full Reaper, true, but Ramsey's apparent lack of concern at Maura's shadow-hopping powers surprised me. He sent Seth to keep an eye on the campers and then beckoned Maura to his office.

"Did the campers manage to get their story straight?" I asked him in an undertone. "Or are you arresting them?"

"No, but I'll see if the Reaper backs up their stories."

"My name's Maura," she said. "For the record."

Ramsey backed through the door to his office. "We'll talk in here. Robin, you wait outside."

"Wait."

I took an indignant step back as Maura elbowed her way past me and let Ramsey usher her into his office. He then closed the door, leaving me to wait with Tansy and the other suspects. Oh, and Maura's brother, who floated behind the desk, blowing on the back of Julian's head.

"There's a ghost behind you," I told the receptionist. "If you're wondering who keeps moving things around."

He jumped out of his seat. "A ghost? I'll get the sage."

"Not the scary sort of ghost," I amended. "He's here with one of the suspects."

"I take that as an insult," said Mart. "I can be terrifying when I want to be."

"Sure you can." I crouched to speak to Tansy outside my brother's office door. "Can you hear anything interesting?"

"Eavesdropping, are you?" Mart floated right through the door and into my brother's office, where I heard a distinct pause in their conversation.

"I told you my brother can't be contained," Maura's voice said from behind the door. "He was also with me in the forest, so he saw everything too."

"What exactly *did* you see?" Ramsey's voice was loud enough that I could hear him if I pressed my ear to the wooden surface.

"Nothing," she said. "I told you, I was looking for a ghost and ran into your sister instead."

"You didn't see or hear the campers?"

"I don't know any campers," she said. "I didn't even know anyone else was in the woods."

"They're local," Ramsey said. "You aren't."

"No, I'm not," Maura confirmed. "I really didn't see anyone else in the woods. What attacked the campers? Did they see?"

I gave up pretending not to be listening in and nudged the door open. "No, they didn't see anything because it went pitch-black. Is that a Reaper ability, by any chance?"

Ramsey's jaw tightened when I stepped in. "I thought I told you to stay outside."

"You said the same to her brother, and he's here." I pointed at Mart, who was hovering upside down above Ramsey's filing cabinets. "Do *you* know if Reapers can make it go pitch-black without using a spell?"

"We can," Maura said, "but so can a lot of creatures from the afterworld."

Afterworld. My blood chilled. "You think a monster from the afterworld killed that guy?"

"If it did, I had nothing to do with it," she replied.

"Are you sure about that?" Ramsey side-eyed her. "I don't think you're being honest."

"If anyone's being dishonest, it's your campers," Maura said. "If they *did* get attacked by a beast from the afterworld, someone must have summoned it in the first place."

"They're shifters," Ramsey said. "They can't use magic. *You* can."

"Then someone else did," Maura said, not missing a beat. "There'll be proof in the forest, I'm sure, near the site of the attack."

"I certainly intend to search the woods," said Ramsey, "but I can't rule you out as a possible suspect, especially given your talents."

"My talents include banishing afterworld creatures, which means I can find the culprit myself," she said. "What do you think?"

"Absolutely not," said Ramsey. "Until we find proof suggesting otherwise, you'll remain a suspect."

Her brows rose at his sharp tone. "If you find proof that someone used a summoning spell, it would rule me out. I don't *need* any props to summon a monster from the afterworld."

"You're a rogue Reaper, aren't you?" Ramsey said. "If you were legitimate, you wouldn't be outside of your region. You also wouldn't be travelling with a ghost."

"Well observed," Maura said. "I'm not a rogue. Do you see me carrying a scythe?"

"She has a point," I ventured. "Anyway, rogue Reapers aren't supposed to be our responsibility, are they?"

Wasn't there some kind of Reaper Council who handled that kind of thing? Maura's mouth twitched in annoyance, suggesting I'd guessed right, but Ramsey refused to relent.

"I'll call the necessary authorities if I need to, but it *is* my responsibility to find the murderer, whether they be human or otherwise. Come with me, Reaper," he ordered.

"Ramsey." I stepped aside as he circled the desk and pushed the office door open. "You're not locking her up, are you?"

"She can stay in a holding cell until I can verify her innocence."

"Why not look for the proof first?" I asked.

Maura could step through the shadows, so a cell wouldn't be able to keep her contained. Ramsey ought to know better, and when he ignored my question, I gave Maura an apologetic look.

"He's like this with everyone. Humour him and you'll be out before you know it," I said.

"If you say so." Maura followed Ramsey out of the office, while Mart pulled faces at my brother's retreating back.

I, meanwhile, turned to my familiar. "If you ask me, he'll

have to go back on that decision. It sounds like a Reaper might be exactly what we need on our side."

"I don't want to make friends with a Reaper," Tansy muttered. "But I bet we can find the proof ourselves."

"You read my mind."

5

Ramsey must have figured out my intentions, because I found Seth and another officer blocking the path into the woods.

"Oh, come on." I gave Seth an eye roll in the hopes that he'd agree how ridiculous my brother was being. "I'm Head Witch. It's not dangerous for me to walk in the woods, and we're nowhere near the crime scene."

"Orders are orders," said the female shifter who accompanied him, a blond woman with a stern demeanour. "We're not to move."

Seth didn't look as thrilled, but he remained firm. "That's right. Sorry, Robin."

"Are you stopping all shifters from using the woods now?" I directed my question at his companion. "And coven members? Would you prevent my mother from entering?"

"Yes," said the blond woman, unconvincingly.

"Come on, really. Be honest."

Seth shifted on his feet. "I can't let you go and look around the crime scene, and that's your plan, isn't it?"

"I never said anything of the sort."

Out of the corner of my eye, I glimpsed Tansy scaling a tree without either of them noticing so much as a twitch of her fluffy tail. If all else failed, she'd be able to sniff out any traces of a summoning spell, but I'd prefer not to send my familiar into the Wildwood alone with a potential killer on the loose.

"There's no other reason for you to be here," said the blond female officer. "Go on home."

"My dad lives on the other side of the forest. Also, my family's house is nearby. Those are both good reasons for me to be here."

I knew better than to think that would convince them to ignore my brother's orders, though. I didn't command enough respect, and while I almost wanted to try walking past with my sceptre in hand just to see what they'd do, I'd have to settle for letting Tansy do the exploring instead. When I surreptitiously looked in her direction, I saw a distinctly *human*-shaped figure ducking out of sight behind a tree.

Well, well. I wasn't the only one trying to get into the woods.

"You there." Seth followed my gaze and spied the newcomer too. "You can't be here."

We both did a double take when the trespasser glanced back over her shoulder, which revealed her face. *Maura.* She must have used her shadowy power to sneak out of the holding cells without my brother noticing her escape.

"What are you doing here?" demanded the blond officer. "You're supposed to be in the holding cells."

Instead of answering, Maura vanished. This time I watched carefully and saw the shadows at her feet rise and swallow her whole, leaving no traces behind.

"Where'd she go?" asked Seth blankly.

"If I had to guess"—I stepped around the two officers,

eyes on the spot where Maura had vanished—"she went back to the scene of the crime."

"You shouldn't be in here either." The blond woman swivelled towards me, but I was already picking up speed. "Hey—where are you going?"

"To find her."

Sceptre in hand, I walked towards the spot where Maura had been, ignoring the protests of the officers behind me. They'd be able to catch me up with relative ease, but I was going by the assumption that they'd be reluctant to risk grabbing the Head Witch in case I used the sceptre on them. Or so I hoped, if just because it wouldn't bode well for the next person to get the job if I caused everyone in town to lose respect for the title altogether.

I might not be able to match a Reaper's ability to hop through the shadows, but I could walk fast when I wanted, and I had the advantage of knowing where the crime scene was too. Tansy helped, scampering through the treetops above my head, and we soon reached the strewn remains of the campers' tents. Given the absence of any officers, Ramsey hadn't had time to send anyone to the scene. *He certainly had time to stop* me *getting here, though.*

I spotted Maura studying the shifters' tracks in the mud while her brother careened in the background, and she straightened up when she saw me.

"I'm only here to look for traces of the summoning spell, I swear. You don't have to turn me in again," she said.

"I don't need to." I jogged to the clearing's edge, while Tansy scaled a nearby tree to get a squirrel's-eye view of the scene from above. "I'm here for the same reason, but those officers are right behind me. Fair warning."

"Figures." She peered underneath some bushes. "I can't see any signs that anyone used a summoning spell at the campsite, so at least they had that much sense."

"You really think one of the campers summoned the monster themselves?" I asked. "I thought shifters couldn't use magic."

"Maybe one of them's a wizard in disguise." She crouched down and picked up a discarded shoe that one of the campers had left behind. "Or they have very reckless friends."

"I guess." I hadn't asked Ramsey for the details of how their story had come together, but I'd been more concerned with not letting Maura out of my sight at the time. "You do realise my brother is even less likely to let you help him after you've given him the slip?"

"Do you really think he was going to let me help? Be realistic."

"Fair."

I crossed the clearing myself, scanning the ground for any signs of a summoning spell that Maura might have missed. I knew what to look for, thanks to the incident when we'd banished the monster the Henbanes had summoned into the woods a few weeks ago, but I didn't see or smell any sage.

It couldn't have been them. The campers didn't have a connection to the covens. *A monster from the afterworld... were they just in the wrong place at the wrong time?*

Rustling sounded, and a moment later, Ramsey came running into view, looking considerably more dishevelled than I'd seen him earlier.

"How did I know I'd find you in the company of our escaped prisoner, Robin?"

Maura gave a resigned shrug. "I didn't think I was a prisoner."

"Don't look at me," I said to my brother. "I had nothing to do with you losing one of your prisoners. I wanted to have a look around on my own."

Ramsey scowled. "I can believe *that*, Robin, but Maura—

you have some nerve coming back to the scene of the crime after escaping the holding cells."

I glimpsed the other two officers behind my brother and figured they must have steered him in the right direction. Typical.

"I know," Maura said. "I figured it'd be quicker if I found the site of the summoning myself rather than letting your officers blunder around the forest. You're free to escort me back into jail if you'd rather do this the slow way."

Ramsey's expression suggested he was seriously considering locking her up for real this time. "It doesn't look like you've found anything to me."

"There's no evidence of a summoning here at the campsite," said Maura, "but that doesn't mean it isn't elsewhere in the woods. Do your officers know what to look for?"

"We know enough." Ramsey turned to the other officers. "Take her back to her cell. If she tries to run again, act accordingly."

"Understood." Seth stepped forward, producing a pair of handcuffs.

Maura gave a pronounced sigh, holding out her hands. "This is a waste of time, you know."

"Go with them," I told her. "I'll stay here and look around. I know what a summoning spell looks like."

"I can see things with my Reaper eyes that nobody else can."

From her tone, she knew she was beaten, though, and she didn't attempt to escape through the shadows. Not even when the officers flanked her and then steered Maura away under Ramsey's watchful eye. Mart trailed along behind them, making obscene gestures.

"Please don't tell me to leave too," I said to my brother. "Your officers weren't even searching the crime scene when I got here, and I *do* know what a summoning spell looks like."

I might have added that my entire purpose of being chosen as Head Witch was to fight against some unknown enemy, and while the beast that had attacked those campers might not be the same as the last time the afterworld had threatened my life, I'd be a fool to ignore the possible connection.

"I'm aware of that," said Ramsey. "That's why I'm here, but I won't allow a suspect to run around the woods."

"You're here to look around the crime scene?" I blinked in surprise. "I thought you were talking to the campers."

"I already questioned them."

He strode past me towards the ruined tents, which I took as an invitation to stay. While part of me was surprised he'd caved in so easily, Maura made me look positively coopera-tive by comparison.

"What did they have to say?" I asked Ramsey. "Did the campers have a coherent story, or were they all confused?"

"Their stories did add up collectively, assuming they told the truth," he replied. "The story is that they were all sitting outside their tents this morning when it went completely dark. They panicked and scattered, shifting into their animal forms, and none of them saw how their friend was killed."

"You had your officers remove the body?"

"I did, yes," he said. "They were going to come back to look around, but evidently Maura decided to get in there first."

"Did any of the campers seem to be hiding something, like Maura suggested?" I queried. "Or is it more likely that they were just unlucky bystanders who happened to be in the forest when someone was up to nefarious deeds?"

"Maura looks more guilty than all three of them put together."

Ramsey reached the end of the clearing, where the body had been found. Police tape had been tied between two trees, but I wouldn't otherwise have known there'd been anyone lying dead in the bushes not an hour earlier.

I joined him. "A Reaper trying to avoid attention isn't going to summon a monster and set it upon a group of campers."

"She didn't give the impression of someone trying to avoid attention."

He crouched beside the bushes, pulling out his wand. Did he expect to have to face the creature himself? The last one had taken half the coven's combined efforts to banish back to the afterworld—not to mention several Head Witches, including me. At least I'd brought the sceptre this time, but its purple glow didn't reveal anything else in the spot where the body had lain.

"Maybe we should have asked a shifter to come with us," I remarked. "They have enhanced senses. They'd be able to sniff out if there was any sage buried in the bushes nearby."

The main herb used to summon or banish ghosts had a distinctive smell, but my less attuned senses were unable to pick out a particular plant amid the general scents of leaves and damp soil. I beckoned Tansy over, but she shook her head.

"I can't smell anything except badger shifter, and… cold," Tansy said.

"Cold as in afterworld-cold?" I asked.

It was a bit cooler in the forest than out in the open, but I hadn't thought the woods had the same creepy vibe as the last time there'd been a monster in here. Animals could pick up on necromancy vibes better than humans could, though, so I'd trust Tansy's word.

"I don't think so." She gave a shiver and then sniffed at the bushes. "It doesn't smell the same as the last monster. I don't smell anything living aside from humans and badger shifters."

"Weird." I faced Ramsey. "Maura's Reaper abilities might be able to track the creature's location, you know."

"She's a suspect, Robin," he said. "And her antics have put me in a difficult position. I don't need my officers questioning my ability to keep my suspects contained."

"I doubt they've ever encountered a suspect that can literally walk through the shadows," I said. "Are you keeping the campers in the holding cells too?"

"No," he said. "They've given me their stories, and we found nothing at the scene of the attack to suggest one of them was involved in their friend's death."

"What about the body?" I asked. "Maybe examining it will turn up some clues about what attacked them."

"That's not your job or mine," he replied. "The body will certainly be examined, but it'll take time."

"You aren't worried that there's a monster out here in the woods that won't wait to be identified before it strikes again?"

Instead of answering, his gaze roved over the area, where churned-up mud showed what appeared to be a mixture of human and animal footprints. Wishing I'd brought my camera, I snapped a few photos on my phone instead.

"Robin," he said. "That isn't necessary. My people have already taken pictures of the prints to identify."

"Good," I said. "I just wanted to compare the prints to the last time. I don't think it's a Ghast, but if we can deal with it in the same way—"

"I knew I shouldn't have let you come back to the crime scene." He pinched the bridge of his nose. "It's not part of your role as Head Witch to banish a dangerous monster, assuming there is one."

"Then whose job is it?" I challenged. "It took several people to entrap and banish the Ghast, and if you exclude me *and* Maura from helping out, someone might get hurt."

"You can't banish it single-handedly either," he replied. "If it isn't the same beast as the last time, we need to find out what it is before we can come up with a strategy. I'll have my officers closely watch the forest in the meantime."

"What if it *is* Maura?" I didn't think it was, but I was curious to hear his response.

"Regardless," he said, "I don't trust her an inch, and if she escapes her cell a second time, I'll have to take more severe steps to secure her."

"You know she's staying in the cell out of goodwill, don't you?" I told him. "She can get out with her eyes closed. And her brother can't be contained at all."

"I don't think Maura did this," Tansy piped up. "I *do* think she's not being honest about this ghost she's chasing."

"Yes, and I intend to ask her about that," Ramsey said. "When I question her."

"Is that the plan?"

"Yes." He turned away. "I'll question her thoroughly and then decide if she merits further punishment."

"What about her brother?"

"Him, too, if he's around." He continued to stride down the path with his back to the clearing. "Before you ask, no, you can't sit in on the questioning."

Figures. "Good luck keeping her inside a cell until then."

He vanished amid the trees, while I debated continuing my search alone. I wasn't familiar with this part of the Wildwood, though, and I'd need a shifter's fine-tuned senses to pick out a particular herb above the pungent smell of badger.

"I told you they stink," Tansy said, when I mentioned this. "You're not staying in here, are you?"

"No, but I'm not going home."

My mother would no doubt be waiting with a lecture on not interfering in police investigations, and I needed to update Rowan on the situation after I'd taken off out of the café earlier. I should probably call Harvey at some point, too, but he'd still be at flight practise, and I didn't need to ruin his afternoon with news of another murder in the woods.

"You're not going to see your dad?" Tansy sat on my shoulder to ride back through the forest.

"I'll text him." He didn't need more bad news from me today, and honestly, I wouldn't blame Jessica for wanting to move out of the Wildwood altogether if there was some kind of nasty afterworld beastie prowling around.

And just how did it kill that guy without touching him?

"Did his friends poison him, I wonder?" I asked Tansy. "That would explain why there wasn't a mark on him."

She shivered, tail fur brushing my ear. "We both know someone else who was fond of using poison."

Aunt Shannon. "Or selling it. If not her, you don't think another Henbane witch might have got ideas?"

"Your guess is as good as mine." She bounded off my shoulder to chase a magpie—luckily, not my aunt's familiar—and then bounded back to my side. "The Henbanes got slapped down pretty hard, and their leader is in jail, but I bet the ones left would love to oust you from your position as Head Witch."

"You'd think they'd have learned their lesson from their last brush with amateur necromancy."

As we reached a more familiar path, the birdsong in the trees made me aware of how comparatively silent the clearing had been. Not a good sign.

"Or Maura's right and one of the campers is secretly a wizard," added Tansy.

"In a badger suit?" Nope, it didn't add up. "I wish I'd been able to listen in on their questioning. And Maura's, come to that."

"He did let you help him search the clearing. That's progress."

"Yeah." With my brother, it was usually a case of two steps forward, one step backwards. "He ought to know that anyone who sends a monster into the Wildwood is a threat to our family even if we're not the intended targets."

"I bet we are," said Tansy. "I also bet Maura knows what kind of monster it is."

That's what I thought too. "He should question her today and then let her go. She's not going to be intimidated at all by the notion of sitting in a holding cell all night."

"She said she wanted to stay in town regardless of whether the police keep her overnight or not," Tansy reminded me. "Either she'll camp in the woods or book into one of the inns."

"Fair point." We didn't exactly have a ton of accommodation options for tourists, which Ramsey knew, so it wouldn't be impossible for him to keep an eye on her without needing to lock her in a cell. "She didn't strike me as the sort of person who'd come here just to stir up trouble for the sake of it. She came for a reason."

Yet trouble was bound to follow her. Of that, I was certain.

6

An evening of playing video games with Rowan was a good way to distract me from the attack in the forest, though we also spent some time talking over theories about what might have been responsible for the shifter's death and whether Maura had given the police the slip again. I didn't hear any disturbances from the direction of the police station, so I assumed she hadn't.

I got back late enough that I managed to avoid a chat with my mother, too, but I came downstairs the following morning to find both her and Ramsey sitting at the kitchen table. Prickles the hedgehog occupied his usual spot on the tabletop, while his owner's uniform indicated that he intended to go back to the office again today.

"Hey, Ramsey," I said, receiving a grunt in answer. "Hey, Mum."

Mum didn't lift her head from the newspaper she was reading. "I'm glad to see you've stopped avoiding me, Robin."

"You were at the office the last time I came home," I pointed out. "What were you doing that couldn't wait until tomorrow morning?"

"Sorting out paperwork from the last mess you presided over," she said snippily. "I'd have thought you'd think twice before interfering with yet another police investigation."

I raised a brow at Ramsey. "Did you tell her *you* were the one who invited me to look around the crime scene?"

My brother ignored me and refilled his coffee mug, while Mum rose to her feet.

"I do hope you don't plan to do any more investigating today. You have a week at the office to prepare for, in case you've forgotten," Mum said.

"I haven't forgotten."

I'd thought Mum had agreed to stop reprimanding me for what I did in my free time at the weekends, though admittedly, murder investigations hadn't been part of that discussion. Yes, I ought to have told her sooner, but she'd have reacted the exact same if I'd sought her out yesterday instead of going to Rowan's place. There was no winning.

"It's also my job to keep an eye out for potential trouble that might implicate the coven," I said as I loaded my plate. "Since I was the target of the last monster from the afterworld to be set loose in the forest, you can hardly blame me for wanting to make sure we don't have a repeat performance."

Mum walked away from the table. "There's a difference between keeping an eye on the situation and elbowing your way in where you aren't needed."

"Ouch." That stung, I had to admit. I'd thought that I *had* been needed the last time, though I'd also been the target to begin with. Also, it would have been nice if my brother stood up for me for once. "Did Ramsey tell you I brought in the suspect I found wandering around the woods?"

"Exactly," Tansy piped up, hopping onto the table. "If not for us, you'd never have known Maura *was* a suspect."

"The Reaper." Mum paused, her hand on the door. "On

that subject, the rest of the coven needs to know there's a Reaper present in Wildwood Heath. Should the subject arise at tomorrow's meeting, you need to prepare a response."

"You really want Grandma to know there's a Reaper in town?" I queried. "She'll upend my office in protest."

"Have you considered that might be the reason the Reaper came to town?" Mum's nostrils flared. "To silence the former Head Witch?"

I stifled a snort. "Good luck to anyone who tries to silence Grandma. Anyway, Maura seems to have trouble controlling the ghost of her own brother, let alone anyone else."

Not typical of a Reaper. By now, I was certain she wasn't the one who'd set loose whatever had attacked those campers, but that didn't mean she'd been entirely truthful with us. It remained to be seen whether a night in the holding cells had convinced her to loosen her tongue… or if she'd made another escape attempt.

Mum walked out of the room, and I returned to my meal, while Tansy stole the crusts off my toast and scampered around the table to the general annoyance of Prickles the hedgehog.

"You should have told her sooner," Ramsey said. "Rather than sneaking out of the house to play games with your cousin."

"There was no sneaking involved." I chewed a mouthful of toast. "You know Mum was at the office all day. If you ask me, she's been listening to Grandma's conspiracy theories. You don't seriously think the Reaper came all the way here to get rid of her ghost, do you?"

"It's not implausible," said Ramsey, "but no, I don't think that's why the Reaper is here."

"Did she behave herself last night?" I reached for another slice of toast. "She didn't try to escape again?"

"No." He finished his coffee. "She kept to her word, but

she also gave away very little of her own intentions. She claimed that she was here for a holiday and that she didn't know the campers were present."

"She told *me* she was looking for a ghost." I washed down my toast with a glass of orange juice. "Did you bring that up with her?"

"Like I said, she wasn't very talkative. Her brother was, but he mostly made inane comments instead of giving any useful information."

"Not that unusual for a ghost." I fed Tansy another crust. "Wait. Is he in the holding cells too?"

"I put sage around one of the holding cells, yes."

I groaned. "Really, Ramsey? That's not going to win either Maura *or* her brother over to your side."

"Winning them over is not my intention," he said. "I had to keep him contained. He kept hassling my staff and causing disruption around the police station."

"Probably because you locked up his sister." I shook my head. "I'm not saying the pair of them can be trusted, but treating them like criminals isn't going to get you any closer to finding out what kind of monster attacked those campers."

"They *are* criminals," he said firmly. "Reapers don't play by the same rules as the rest of us, but they have a rigid code, and I can guarantee that the pair of them are rogues in everything but name."

"Doesn't make them murderers," I said. "I find it difficult to believe a cold-blooded killer would have brought their prankster ghostly brother in tow."

I should have guessed Maura wouldn't respond to my brother's hard-line approach to interrogation. I'd probably made more progress with her when she'd given the police the slip to look around the crime scene than Ramsey had achieved from a night in the holding cells... not that he'd appreciate me pointing that out. As usual, I'd have to wait for him to change his mind on his own schedule.

Ramsey got up to leave, and I hastened to put forward my other theory. "Have you thought any more about having a look around the Henbane Coven's house?"

"The police confiscated everything they had," he replied. "We searched thoroughly."

"I know their leader is in jail, but it's not implausible that she left instructions for someone else." Admittedly, the last apprentice she'd taught had *died* in the process of following her guidance, but the Henbanes were the last people in town who'd meddled with necromancy. Even Aunt Shannon wouldn't have touched it. "You know… you know what I saw in the Seeing Stone."

Ramsey's jaw tensed. "Yes, and you aren't ready for that vision to come to pass yet."

"Oh, thanks." Heat rushed to my face. "I'm not saying I'm an expert, but it took several Head Witches to banish the Ghast, and I don't see anyone else volunteering to back me up." Like it or not, I might need the Reaper's assistance if I didn't want to find myself in the afterworld in a more permanent manner.

He dropped his gaze, seemingly realising he'd hit a nerve. "That's exactly why I think we need to tread carefully."

"Talking to the remaining Henbanes counts as treading carefully," I pointed out. "Their leader's behind bars, and as you pointed out yourself, the police confiscated anything dangerous they possessed. There's no harm in asking a few questions at their headquarters."

"She's right." Tansy leapt off the table onto Ramsey's forearm, scampering up to his shoulder to whisper in his ear. "You know she is."

He dislodged her with a gentle shake of his arm. "Fine. I

don't have to be in the office for another hour, so I can pay the Henbanes a visit."

He actually said yes? Maybe the prospect appealed more than another round of questioning with a stubborn Reaper, but I wasn't complaining that he'd finally listened. While Tansy bounded ahead of me, Prickles took her place on Ramsey's shoulder and gave me a reproachful look. I hid a smile, checking that Mum was too busy presiding over her prizewinning rosebushes in the back garden to raise a fuss about me accompanying my brother.

"What was she actually doing at the office yesterday?" I asked Ramsey as we walked out of the house. "I don't know what she can possibly have left to 'clean up' in the aftermath of the attack on the Head Witches. I already sent letters of formal apology to all of them."

"It pays to be prepared." He closed the front door and strode ahead, down the cul-de-sac where our coven's head-quarters stood next door to our major rival's.

As we neared, the door to our own headquarters opened, and none other than Aunt Shannon walked out. *What was she doing in there?* She was hardly the type to work at the week-end, and her presence instantly raised my suspicions.

Seeing our approach, she gave a curt nod. "Head Witch."

"Hello, Aunt Shannon," I said brightly. "It's a lovely morning, isn't it?"

She walked past with her nose in the air, while Ramsey side-eyed me. "You shouldn't bait her, Robin."

"She's already angry with me," I muttered. "I wonder if *she's* the one who's dabbling in necromancy?"

"Didn't we already go through that theory and reject it?"

"Last time we did," I acknowledged, "but that was before we caught her peddling illegal potions on the black market."

"Yes, but I confiscated anything that might have been remotely dangerous from her office."

"Bet she loved that." Aunt Shannon had as few morals as the Henbanes did, but she also had more sense than to dabble in necromancy. Selling illegal potions wasn't on the same level, danger-wise… And now that I thought on the subject, it had been the Henbanes who'd brewed the potions in the first place. They might be low on supplies, but summoning a monster from the afterworld didn't require many more props than a handful of common herbs that were easy to obtain.

The Henbanes' headquarters stood next to our own, a smaller building that was considerably less well-kept, with overgrown gardens and the curtains drawn across the windows. The last time I'd checked, they hadn't chosen a new leader yet, and had spent the past few weeks arguing back and forth over who was the best option.

Ramsey rapped on the door, and it swung inward, revealing Leona, Tiffany's former apprentice. Her red hair was in disarray, and her robes were covered in dirt, for some reason. Maybe she'd been digging an escape tunnel to get away from the other witches' bickering over the contenders for their coven's leadership. As a magical dud, Leona certainly wouldn't have been a potential contender.

"Head Witch," she said, her tone inflectionless. "What do you want?"

Honestly, she could stand to be a little friendlier. Yes, I'd seen to her mentor's arrest, but if I hadn't, she might have died too. Tiffany had already proven that she was more than happy to sacrifice her apprentices to get her way.

"I don't know if you heard about the incident in the forest yesterday…" I began, but she cut through me.

"What are you trying to blame us for this time?" Leona grouched. "We haven't been in the forest."

"There was an attack," I went on. "Some camping badger

shifters were attacked by a monster summoned by necromancy."

Her jaw twitched. "Did you forget I can't use magic?"

"The rest of your coven can." What was her problem today? "Are you sure Tiffany didn't leave instructions behind?"

Her eyes narrowed. "We're busy picking a new leader and undoing the damage you did to us. We don't have time to mess around in the forest."

"I'm not the one who left my former apprentice for dead." Had she shifted the blame onto my coven instead of her own?

"No, but your aunt stole our entire potion stock," she said, "and I don't see you putting an effort into replacing them."

"The potions were illegal," Ramsey said. "As to the leadership contest, I do hope you intend to inform the police when you make a decision."

"And the Head Witch," I added, mostly so that any of her fellow coven members who might be listening in wouldn't assume he outranked me. "Anyway, good luck, I guess."

She closed the door in my face, and I took a step back. "She's decided Tiffany's arrest was our fault, has she?"

"I expected as much," he said. "After losing their leader, their coven had two choices. They either had to disband altogether or find someone else to point the finger of blame at."

I turned away from the door. "You didn't confiscate *all* their potions, did you?"

"There was no telling which of them might have been tampered with."

Meaning yes. "No wonder she's ticked off."

He walked ahead of me. "I didn't expect a confession, at any rate."

"Not from someone who can't use magic." I lowered my voice. "If you ask me, Tiffany herself is the one we ought to ask."

Ramsey gave me a sideways look. "I don't remember giving you permission to talk to a high security prisoner."

"It doesn't have to be me, but it's worth finding out if she knows anything. I can guarantee she won't be able to resist gloating when she finds out."

"I'll consider the matter after I'm done with questioning the Reaper," he said. "Can I trust you not to go wandering into the woods again while I'm at work?"

The cheek of it. "You and I searched the crime scene ourselves, didn't we? I don't remember you complaining then."

"That's precisely why," he said. "We already searched. Any further intervention in the woods might put you in the path of the creature that attacked those campers."

"Assuming it's still at large." I hadn't seen any clues pointing to its location, but the Wildwood covered a vast area, and I didn't have a Reaper's ability to cross large distances by jumping through my own shadow. "Fine, I won't go back into the woods."

I couldn't say the same of Tansy, but she'd disappeared at some point during our altercation with Leona. When we approached the house, I spotted her disappearing into the alley leading to the back garden, presumably to chase some pigeons away from the bird feeder.

An odd whirring noise greeted us inside the hall. I stepped around Carmilla, Grandma's cat, who'd chosen to take a nap in the middle of the hallway again. In the living room, Mum's familiar, Horace, occupied his usual spot on the sofa, but the sound came from elsewhere. I tracked it down to the small home office underneath the stairs that I usually forgot existed; generally, Mum went to her office at the coven's headquarters if she wanted to work at the weekend or in the evenings.

"What are you doing?" I nudged open the door to the

office and spied the source of the whirring—an ancient printer that none of us had used in years. Next to it sat a pile of faded photographs. "Wait—are these the photos of the Ghast's footprints?"

"Yes," she said. "You took photos of the forest this time, too, didn't you?"

"On my phone, not my camera." I picked up the faded prints. "I wondered where those photos disappeared to."

"Take them." She held out a hand for my phone. "I'll print the new ones."

"Erm… okay." It was strange for her to offer to help, but maybe she was trying to make peace with me after our disagreement earlier. "I couldn't see any prints that belonged to anything that wasn't a human or badger."

After I handed her my mobile phone, she plugged it into the printer. "We'll see."

From the hallway, the front door clicked shut, which indicated my brother had headed to the police station. I had no desire to stand awkwardly in a small space with my mother while I waited for the photos to print, so I went looking for my familiar instead.

In the back garden, Piper, my best friend and the family's gardener, was up to her elbows in dirt as she worked on Mum's prizewinning flowers.

"Hey, Robin. Quiet weekend?"

"You heard about the attack in the forest?" I spied my familiar scaling the bird feeder in one of her attempts to outwit the local pigeons.

"Your mother told me." She carefully snipped at a stem. "Is she in the house?"

"Yeah, she's printing photos of the crime scene from my phone."

"She is?" She lifted her head. "Weird of her to get involved."

"She's been in an odd mood all weekend." I watched Tansy chase a grey squirrel off the bird feeder. "That reminds me. I haven't asked the local wildlife if they saw anything in the woods."

"I thought they avoided creepy places." She returned her attention to the rose bushes. "Including your familiar."

"True, but it's not the same as the last time." Catching sight of the squirrel Tansy had chased off, I rose to my feet and called, "Erm, excuse me, did you see anything weird in the forest recently?"

"The forest?" The squirrel halted next to the flowerbed, its tail sticking up. "No—ahh!"

Tansy leapt, causing her quarry to flee for the fence and depart the garden at speed. "And don't come back!"

"Really, Tansy?" I shook my head at my familiar. "We were talking."

"Grey squirrels aren't intelligent enough to be of any use, unlike red squirrels," Tansy said self-importantly.

"If you say so," I said. "Don't you think it's weird that the wildlife returned to the forest so quickly compared to the last time?"

Did that mean the monster was no longer there? If so, where had it gone?

"Isn't that *good* news?" Piper snipped another stem from the roses. "That there's nothing nasty in the woods?"

"Something killed that camper," I said. "Something that left no traces. And there's a Reaper in town."

"There's a *what* in town?" She dropped the gardening tools. "A Reaper?"

"Half Reaper." Mum hadn't told her that part, then. "She claimed she found this town by accident while wandering in the woods."

"Like hell." She gave a shudder. "Reapers go hunting for

trouble. That's their job. Is she staying in one of the local inns?"

"No, she's currently sitting in a cell." Assuming she hadn't made another escape attempt. "My brother didn't appreciate her trying to give him the slip with her creepy shadowy power."

I gave Piper a brief explanation of everything she'd missed, assuming my mother had told her the bare minimum to avoid word spreading to the rest of the coven. Piper knew better than to spread gossip outside of our family, but even the rest of the coven members were bound to have opinions on our visitor.

"Robin." Mum came out of the house, interrupting our conversation. "Are you distracting Piper from her work?"

"Just letting her know about our Reaper friend." I held out my hand to take my phone back from her. "Did you print the photos?"

"Yes, I did." She beckoned me to follow her inside the house, where she handed me three photos of the smudged footprints in the forest.

As I held the fresh photos next to the images of the Ghast's prints, Tansy hopped onto my shoulder to look.

"Those are badger prints," Tansy said.

"All of them?" I'd thought as much myself. "No monster footprints?"

"Nope." Tansy scampered down and ran back into the garden.

Before I joined her, I turned to my mother. "What do you think? Tansy said the wildlife has already returned to the forest, which suggests the monster isn't around."

Mum set her shoulders. "If I had to guess, we're dealing with someone attempting to distract us from our work and frighten us into avoiding the forest."

"You mean a false alarm? How'd that guy drop dead, then?"

"What's up?" Piper approached us, eyeing the photos. "Those are the monster prints?"

"Those are the prints from the last time." I held up the photos for her to see, so she didn't get dirt-stained finger-prints all over them. "And these are from yesterday."

"Weird." She wrinkled her nose. "Did you say it might be a false alarm?"

"Yes," Mum said, "and I'd appreciate it if you went back to work, Piper. You, too, Robin."

"Work?" I echoed.

"Yes, you need to prepare for tomorrow's meeting."

"Already did."

Generally, my sole job at our daily council meetings was to announce the start and the agenda and then leave the other witches to argue themselves into exhaustion. If they had any questions about the Reaper, though, I'd have to wait and see if my brother decided to let her walk free before I figured out how much to tell them.

My phone buzzed with a message from Harvey asking if I wanted to meet up for a lunch date at Were's My Coffee? I replied with a "hell, yes," figuring I'd also have the chance to get another opinion on the photos from him as well as from Rowan.

Whatever my mother thought, I found it hard to believe that the attack was a false alarm. Nothing in my life was ever that simple.

7

W ere's My Coffee? was bustling with customers, but as the café was quieter than the previous day, I managed to claim a table by the counter to wait for Harvey. Rowan smiled at me from where she was serving a shifter I recognised as Dale Longfoot, the guy who'd been a suspect in the last murder case. Upon seeing me near the counter, he startled and muttered, "Head Witch," and I was frankly relieved he didn't bow in deference.

"I wish they wouldn't do that," I said to Rowan in an undertone as Dale walked away. "I'm not even carrying my sceptre."

"I know, right?" She fished out a glass. "The usual?"

"For me, yes, but Harvey might want something else."

As if on cue, I saw him enter the café out of the corner of my eye.

"Also, I have some photos you might want to look at." I handed them over and waved Harvey to come and join us.

Rowan examined the photos one-handed, a furrow in her brow. "What's this supposed to be?"

"Footprints," I replied. "From the last crime scene and this one. Mum and Piper both agree that the second one only has badger and human prints, no monsters."

"I'd have to agree," she said.

Rowan gave me the photos back and busied herself making our drinks while I passed the photos on to Harvey and filled him in on the latest perplexing development.

"There weren't any clearer prints?" He handed the photos back to me across the table when he'd finished examining them.

"Nope." I slid the prints back into my bag. "Mum is assuming the whole thing is a false alarm, but a guy doesn't drop dead for no reason."

Harvey watched as Rowan put our drinks on the table. "Poison? Or did someone curse him?"

I thought back to my chat with Leona. She might not be able to use magic, but poison would have been right up her coven's alley… if I hadn't happened to know the police had confiscated everything Aunt Shannon hadn't already swiped from their stores. Also, it probably wasn't a good idea to discuss the subject inside a café in which someone had actually been poisoned to death a few weeks ago.

"It's possible that the creature jumped straight back into the afterworld after the attack without leaving any prints," I acknowledged, "but that's assuming the shifters' description of everything going completely dark was accurate. If not for there being a Reaper in town, I'd be inclined to think their eyes were playing tricks on them."

Maura might know the truth, but she remained stubbornly close-lipped. How long did my brother plan to keep her contained? It was a miracle she hadn't staged a second escape, but it had rained overnight, and she might have been happier with a roof over her head, even if it belonged to a holding cell.

Harvey and I didn't have any more theories, so we

returned to more pleasant topics for the rest of our lunch date. Rowan stopped by the table to chat whenever she had a spare moment, but after an hour, Harvey rose to his feet.

"I wish I could stay longer, but I have to meet my team for another practise session."

"Already?"

"I have classes all next week so this was the only time we could fit one in," he said apologetically. "I'll call you later?"

"Sure," I said. "I might drop by the jail again and see if I can't change my brother's mind on letting me talk to Maura today."

Rowan was all in favour of that idea. After Harvey had left the café, she whispered to me, "I think Ramsey'll cave in and let her out. It's just a matter of time."

"I can ask if he's changed his mind on talking to Tiffany too." I beckoned to my familiar, who was scrouging crumbs from underneath the tables, and we left the café.

"I have an idea." Tansy scampered up to my shoulder. "Why don't I sneak into the holding cells to see Maura while you're showing your brother those photos?"

"Maura can't understand you," I pointed out. "Nor can Tiffany. You can't question them."

"No, but I can 'accidentally' knock the sage out of the way of the cell where her ghostly brother is imprisoned."

"Right, I forgot about that." My brother must have been annoyed at Mart's antics the previous night if he'd gone to the lengths of locking up a ghost who as well as being incorporeal, hadn't technically broken any laws. "Keep that idea on hold. Don't forget Ramsey can see ghosts too."

Undeterred, Tansy scurried ahead of me and into the police station. Before I could call her back, she streaked across the lobby in a bright-red blur and disappeared inside the holding cells.

My brother came out of his office as the doors closed behind me. "How did I guess you'd be back?"

Crossing the lobby, I sheepishly held up the photos Mum had printed. "Mum thought you might want to look at these."

"She already messaged me and told me the photos are a dead end."

Thanks, Mum. "Not necessarily. Yeah, the prints prove it isn't the same monster as the last time, but *something* killed that guy. Has anyone identified the cause of death yet?"

"Not yet." His attention slid to the door to the holding cells, which Tansy had left slightly open. "Did you send your familiar to spy on the prisoners?"

"No." Busted. "She sent herself, but it's not like they can understand her. They aren't going to give away all their secrets to a squirrel."

"Meaning Tiffany?" He veered towards the door and pushed it further open. Inside one of the holding cells, I saw Maura sitting on a bench, watching as Tansy's fluffy tail disappeared around a corner.

"What's your familiar doing in here?" she asked.

"Good question." I didn't see Mart, so my brother must have locked him in a different part of the prison, no doubt to keep him from talking to his sister from behind bars. "Ramsey—"

"That's enough." Ramsey followed Tansy's path down the corridor, ignoring Maura altogether. "Robin, I'd appreciate it if you kept your familiar under control."

"Good luck with that." Tansy did whatever she liked, and she'd won me a chance to talk to Maura. Entering the holding cells, I asked, "Maura, did you see the police lock up your brother's ghost?"

"Yeah, and he's not best pleased," she said. "He'll haunt the police station for a week when he gets out."

"Believe me, I know all about destructive ghosts." The words slipped out before I could think better of it—I hadn't intended to tell her about my grandmother—and I hastened to change the subject. "Maybe that's what attacked those shifters in the woods."

Wait. A ghost wouldn't leave footprints *or* a scent behind, but they weren't capable of killing someone without leaving a mark on them. Or so I thought. Maura was the expert, not me.

She pushed to her feet and stretched. "Haven't a clue, since I haven't been able to properly look around the forest."

I looked for Ramsey, but he'd pursued Tansy around the corner and wasn't paying me any attention. "Did you tell my brother everything you knew?"

"Your brother needs to chill out," she said. "I get that he's doing a difficult job—my boyfriend is the head of the police force in my own town, so I get it—but I'm not going to be able to help from behind bars."

"You're a stranger," I pointed out. "You're also hiding information from the police."

"There are some things only Reapers understand," she said. "Though it doesn't look like the police have made any progress on their own."

"They do know the beast isn't currently in the woods." I studied her face, but her expression gave nothing away. "And it left no footprints or any other traces. In fact, one might think that the intention was to cause an unnecessary panic, if not for someone being dead."

"I suppose it would look like that, if you can't see with a Reaper's eyes."

Throwing caution to the wind, I lifted the photos to show her them through the cell's bars. "Look at these. What does your Reaper sight show you?"

Her brows shot up. "Those are a Ghast's prints. Was that photo taken in the woods?"

"Not recently." She knew enough to recognise the monster's footprints, but I'd expected as much. "The second photo is of the incident at the weekend."

"Yeah… Those are a human's footprints. And a badger's." She lifted her head. "Who exactly summoned a Ghast? Did they know what they were doing?"

"No, and they ended up dead," I said. "However, we caught the perpetrator who put her up to it, and she's currently locked in a highly secure cell. The police also confiscated every prop her coven had in their possession."

"Robin." Ramsey returned, holding an indignant Tansy in his hand. "Take your familiar and get her out of here. And stop talking to the prisoners."

"When did you plan to let her out?" Resigned, I followed him into the lobby, where he let go of Tansy. My familiar shot across the room like a fluffy bullet, straight through the automatic doors and into the street.

"When she tells me everything she knows."

Assuming she doesn't escape again. "Have you spoken to Tiffany yet?"

"Briefly," he said. "She seems entirely ignorant of the situation."

"Seems," I emphasised. "She's a world-class actress, and she almost certainly gave instructions to the rest of her coven. If you don't believe it's the Henbanes, what do *you* think is going on?"

"I think Maura has an agenda," he said. "I also think the campers aren't entirely innocent of their friend's death. Having said that, it's clear that there's no longer a danger in the forest."

"Oh, that means you're going to remove your officers from guarding the paths?" I smiled. "Good. I just got into the habit of jogging in the woods, and I'd hate to have to give it up."

"Robin." He sighed. "The reports on the cause of death will be in by tomorrow, but I'd appreciate it if you kept away from here until then. That means your familiar too."

"I'll tell her." When I asked if she'd seen Maura's ghostly brother.

I left the police station, and I stopped dead in my tracks when Mart himself floated across my path with a cheery wave. I looked for the culprit and saw Tansy perched on the gutter above, looking incredibly pleased with herself.

"Get away from the police station," I told Mart. "Someone will see you."

"Only if they can see ghosts." He gave the doors a rude gesture. "I can't believe they locked me up."

"I assume he wanted to avoid you helping your sister escape," I said. "Isn't that right, Tansy?"

"I thought he'd be able to help us," she said huffily. "Your brother didn't need to manhandle me."

"He's under a lot of stress." Not that that was anything new. To Mart, I said, "Wait, are *you* a Reaper?"

"It runs in the family, so yes." He lifted his chin. "Being dead doesn't make me any less awesome."

"Right." *Maybe I can work with that.* "If there was a sign in the forest that only a Reaper could see, would it be visible to you?"

"You want me to help you search for your elusive beastie?" he asked. "If so, it'll cost you."

"You want me to pay you?" Since when did ghosts demand payment? "What, in cash?"

"Maybe." A grin appeared on his face. "I usually take payment in the form of hot showers."

"You want a hot shower?" Even by ghost standards, that was weird. "You can't feel anything, can you?"

He made a shocked noise. "How dare you. I'm hurt."

As he floated away down the street, I watched for a bewildered instant before hurrying to catch up, while Tansy scurried along the gutters above my head.

"Wait!" I caught up to him outside the local shop, causing several people to turn in my direction. I lowered my voice, hoping people would think I was talking to my familiar rather than conversing with a ghost. "I'm sorry if I upset you, but I've never met a ghost who wants to be paid before. Let alone in showers."

Grandma wanted to claim my sceptre, of course, but the sceptre had originally been hers, and half the time she was in denial about being dead. This guy was undeniably a little touchy at the subject, too, but I didn't know how to negotiate with a spirit who wasn't related to me.

Mart pouted. "I don't think it's unreasonable to ask for a shower. I feel all grimy after being in that cell for hours."

"You don't have a speck of dirt on you." I had an inkling I might be fighting a losing battle, but I didn't want to imagine how my mother would react if I let a ghost use her shower.

"Then I'll take my Reaper skills elsewhere." He spun around and floated away down the high street.

I quickened my pace, determined to keep him within my sight. "What about your sister? Don't you want me to help her out?"

"She didn't need help getting out of her cell the last time," he said over his shoulder.

Well, true. "She'll only end up in more trouble if she pulls another disappearing act. I realise she has her reasons, but she's not exactly proving herself a paragon of trustworthiness."

"Only because your brother won't let her," he said. "What *is* his problem?"

"He likes to be in control," I said. "He also likes things to be orderly. Which is about the opposite of you and your sister."

He snorted. "I'm way more fun than she is. She's the boring sibling."

"Where are you even going?" I dodged several passers-by as he took a sharp turn off the high street and into the quieter part of Wildwood Heath.

"None of your business."

"You're going to look around the forest, aren't you?" I tilted my head. "Would you object if I tagged along?"

"I'd still expect payment." He floated onward through the streets until we came within sight of one of many entrances to the woodland. "It's only fair."

"You're lucky the other officers patrolling the forest can't see ghosts."

From what I could see of the forest entrance ahead of us, they'd already left. Understandable, given the lack of any proof of a monster roaming the woods.

"Aren't you Head Witch?" Mart picked up speed again. "You should be able to do whatever you like, even when you don't have that shiny stick of yours."

"No—not at all." I caught up with him at the entrance to the forest. "The Head Witch doesn't have supreme authority. Nobody does. Also, it was kind of an accident that I got chosen."

Mum would be livid if she overheard me telling him that, but I didn't believe he or Maura might be plotting to unseat me. Not only had they plainly had no idea I was Head Witch when they'd shown up, they weren't involved in any covens, especially mine. Even if it turned out they'd been behind the badger shifter's death after all, it wasn't personal.

"Ooh, I want to hear that story," Mart said.

"I'll tell you," I said, "if you help me look for clues in the forest. How does that sound?"

"Nice try. I still want the shower."

He was persistent, I'd give him that. "I'm not being unreasonable. My mother would throw a fit if you went into our house to use our shower."

"You still live with your mother?" He laughed, while I ducked under a low-hanging branch across the entrance to the woods.

"Under duress." I shouldn't have told him *that*, either. "The house is our coven's ancestral home, and I'm only there temporarily."

He continued to laugh under his breath as we entered the forest proper. "Doesn't the Head Witch get her own shower?"

I did have an en suite bathroom, but like hell was I letting him anywhere near it. "We'll revisit that one later."

"Too late." He zoomed off, swiftly vanishing among the trees with one final cackle.

Wonderful. "Tansy—can you follow him?"

"Way ahead of you," she called down from the treetops.

I hadn't exactly dressed for running in the woods, so I settled for a fast walk as I followed my familiar's path. The forest was quiet and peaceful, but not in a creepy manner, and honestly, I was almost inclined to believe my mother's claim that the whole thing had been a false alarm. If not for the remaining uncertainty surrounding the shifter's death.

As we neared the part of the forest that backed to my mother's house, I briefly debated smuggling Mart into the house after all. If my mother went to the office again, I might be able to get away with running a quick shower for a needy ghost, but I didn't need to tick off my mother any further by accidentally flooding the house. I was pretty sure ghosts couldn't turn taps on or off, after all.

I came to a halt when Mart surfaced from the bushes, a triumphant expression on his face.

"I told you so. I found proof that someone was up to no good in the forest," he said.

"You did?" I looked behind him, but I didn't see anything but oak trees and sunbeams shining through the canopy onto a carpet of leaves. "Where?"

"I won't show you unless you keep your word," he said. "One hot shower."

"I never gave you my word in the first place." A streak of red showed Tansy scampering across from me, near— "Wait —you found evidence right behind our house?"

"Stop right there!" he protested, but I ran to catch up to my familiar near a set of bushes behind Mum's house. The distinct smell of sage wafted out, and Tansy's tail stuck up in agitation.

"This was a summoning circle," she said. "I can smell it."

My skin chilled. Maura's guess that someone had disposed of the evidence in the forest had been dead-on— and behind my mother's house, no less. All my suspicions about the Henbanes returned tenfold. "Right. I'll tell Mum."

"Hey!" Mart reappeared, scowling. "I'm the one who found this. I demand compensation."

"Fine, I'll book you a hotel room," I said distractedly. "Trust me, you don't want my mother finding you messing with the shower in her house. Being a ghost won't make you immune to whatever she might do to you in retaliation. She's the head of our coven for a reason."

"I thought you were coven leader."

"No, I'm just Head Witch." I lowered my voice, conscious of Aunt Shannon's house next door to Mum's. *Was it she who summoned something from the afterworld?* No, she wouldn't have disposed of the evidence so close to her own property, assuming she'd taken the risk to begin with.

"Where are you going?" Mart tailed me to the back gate to Mum's house, which I opened, intending to take a short cut through the garden. "I can't believe you still live with your mother."

"Look, I got dragged back here when the Head Witch thing happened," I told him. "I'll be gone soon, so there was no point in renting anywhere else."

"What?" The question came from Piper, who watched us enter the garden, her expression baffled and hurt. *Ack. I didn't know she could hear us.*

"Er… You can't see ghosts, can you?" I asked.

"You know I can't." She frowned. "What does that have to do with anything?"

"That's who I was talking to." I gestured to Mart, who pulled a face at her.

Piper's expression remained bewildered. "I thought you were talking to Tansy."

"Sorry."

"Don't worry about it." She dropped her gaze. "I knew—I mean, I knew you didn't want to stay here, but I didn't expect it to be that soon."

"It's not. I mean, it won't be." Guilt warmed my face. I hadn't mentioned my plans to leave town for a while, but I also hadn't realised that everyone had defaulted to assuming I would stay. Except my family, but that went without saying. "A ghost decided to tease me about living with my mother— Mart, stop!"

He approached the house at speed, zooming straight through Mum's flowerbeds.

Piper stared as I made to follow him. "Robin, *what* is going on?"

"The ghost wants to take a shower. Don't ask."

"All right, but tell me everything later, won't you?"

"I will."

I reached the back door and ran inside—too late. A bright flash dazzled my eyes, and I glimpsed Mart's ghostly form disappearing through the closed front door and out of sight.

Mum peered out of her office, her wand in her hand. "Did you bring that ghost into the house, Robin?"

"Definitely not," I said firmly. "But you should know we found evidence of a summoning spell in the forest. Guess it's not a hoax after all."

8

———

"I don't see anything," the officer said, as I pointed to the pile of sage in the bushes and the hastily covered-up remnants of a summoning circle.

I used my sceptre for emphasis, but the blond officer—I'd finally got her name, Shana—appeared unimpressed.

"That is a summoning spell," I said.

Even Mum had reluctantly believed me when I'd given her the bad news, but she'd wanted the police to give their opinion before she started pointing fingers.

"Sage is used to summon monsters—or banish them, but I don't think our killer would have been that considerate, do you?"

"There's no proof this sage was used to summon anything," Shana insisted, while Seth paced behind her. He at least was more inclined to listen, but Shana was acting as if the location of the summoning spell was nothing more than a coincidence.

"Do you want to tell my mother that the evidence of a summoning spell near her house is nothing to worry about?" I queried.

Seth winced. "Of course not, but Lady Wildwood herself claimed that there's no proof this was used for a summoning spell, isn't that right?"

No. Unfortunately. Mum hadn't completely let go of her assumption that it was a hoax, though the fact that someone had been messing around with sage behind our house was undeniably a cause for concern. I wished my brother had come instead of sending two of his officers, though he would not be pleased when he found out that the person who'd led us to the evidence was supposed to be locked up. Mart had yet to return after Mum had chased him off, but it would have taken a hell of a lot longer to find the proof without the help of a Reaper. Even a dead one.

"Go home, Head Witch," Shana said. "We can handle this ourselves."

"It doesn't look like you're handling anything," I said. "It looks more like you're choosing to ignore the evidence."

"Of what?"

"Dodgy magic. Messing with the afterworld." The sage alone didn't prove anything, but its proximity to my mother's house made me certain someone had been trying to get our attention. "Seth, what exactly is my brother doing?"

"Paperwork." Seth peered at the bushes. "That *is* sage, though. We'll take note of it."

"Assuming you didn't put it there yourself," added Shana.

"Why would I do that?" What *was* her problem with me? She was a shifter, so it wasn't as if my coven had ticked her off in any way. "I don't need to summon any ghosts. I have one living in my office already."

Not to mention Mart, wherever he was. I assumed he hadn't gone back to the jail to find his sister—or hell, maybe he had. My brother was clearly too occupied with keeping his paperwork up to date to notice anything else.

"Nevertheless," said Shana. "I'd appreciate it if you left the police to do their jobs."

"Shana, be reasonable," Seth said. "She's not wasting our time. If someone's been messing with the afterworld…"

"A group of shifters was attacked. *She* wasn't." Shana indicated me. "Why would the murderer bury the evidence here?"

"I'm wondering the same," I said. "Afterworld monsters aren't exactly easy to control. The last one went on a rampage in the woods and took several Head Witches to bring down. This one might have gone after the shifters by accident."

"Accident or not, someone is dead," she said. "And if I believe your claims that a beast from the afterworld killed that boy, I do hope your family is preparing to take action."

I didn't miss the accusatory note to her voice. *That's what's bugging her.* If my family had been the intended targets, I didn't entirely blame her for being annoyed that one of her own fellow shifters had been killed instead.

"If you want action, ask my brother to let Maura out of the holding cells."

"The Reaper?" Disgust rippled across her face. "Out of the question."

"She's still a suspect," Seth said apologetically. "I'll talk to him…"

"Cheers." I was wasting my time trying to convince Shana, when she was still reluctant to accept that the attack had come from the afterworld at all, but I had zero desire to return home and face Mum's questions about how I'd ended up bargaining with a ghost.

Instead, I veered in the direction of Dad's cottage, figuring that he and the others needed to know that the attack hadn't been a false alarm and someone had genuinely been screwing around with illegal magic in the woods.

Who, though? Given the sage's proximity to our house, I was inclined to pin the blame squarely on the Henbanes, but with Tiffany feigning ignorance and Leona denying her coven's involvement, it would be hard to prove.

With Tansy at my side, I followed the path to my dad's house and rapped on the cottage door.

"Robin!" Dad greeted me with a smile. "What're you doing over here?"

Nothing good. Unfortunately. "Erm… have you seen the police around today?"

"No," he replied. "I thought they left the forest."

"That was before I found evidence of a summoning spell behind my mother's house."

His face fell. "You did?"

"Yeah… I thought you should know," I said. "My brother's dragging his heels on coming to look for himself, so his officers sent me packing without being completely convinced."

"You're not going behind your brother's back, are you?"

"No… not at this precise moment." No point in being less than honest with him. "He locked up the Reaper and her brother—who happens to be a ghost—in the holding cells for hiding information from him. I don't think his approach is going to convince them to change their minds, so I asked the ghost for help."

Dad's brow wrinkled. "How can he have locked up a ghost?"

"Using sage—until my familiar let him out." I nodded to Tansy, who'd begun scampering in front of the living room window to the general entertainment of the small children inside the room. "He helped us find the proof. Maura's brother might be a ghost, but he's just as much of a Reaper as she is."

"I can see why your brother's officers would be a little

sceptical." He smiled when the two kids shrieked in delight at Tansy's antics.

"How are the kids, anyway?" I asked. "I never asked how they were dealing with it all."

"I was worried, but honestly, they seem fine," he commented. "Rambunctious as ever."

"I'm glad they're okay." As I watched, Tansy did a backflip, to a chorus of applause from inside the house. "I don't know if the police are going to block off part of the forest again, but it might be worth avoiding the area around the badger shifters' campsite for the time being."

"Don't worry, Jessica has no intention of taking the kids out into the forest until the coast is clear," he said. "I hope they find the culprit. That poor shifter was only eighteen, Jessica said."

"Yeah… Whereabouts do those badger shifters actually live, do you know?" Not near the coven, so the odds of them being caught in the monster's path by complete accident looked more and more likely.

"Near the playing field, according to Jessica." A knock on the window drew his attention back to the house. "I should go and help Jessica wrangle the kids. Want to come in?"

"I need to see my brother." Not that he'd be willing to listen, but I'd just bring the mood down if I went into the house and started talking about creepy monsters in the forest. "It was nice seeing you, though."

"Anytime." He gave me a hug, while Tansy waved goodbye to the kids and backflipped off the windowsill to my side. "Let me know how tomorrow goes, okay?"

"Tomorrow?" Oh, right. I had to go back to work, and if my mother was to be believed, explain to the council why there was a Reaper in town. "It'd be nice if I could help my brother instead, but hell will freeze over before my mother allows me to skive off work."

"I'm sure Ramsey will be able to get to the bottom of this," he said. "Stay safe."

"I will." Or as safe as possible for a Head Witch who was an apparent target of yet another meddler in illegal magic.

As Dad closed the door, Tansy gave a yelp. I spun on my heel and did a double take when I spied Maura standing behind me, looking for all the world like she'd been there the whole time. "How long have you been eavesdropping?"

"Long enough," she said. "What did you do to put my brother in such a sulk?"

"He offered to help me find clues in the forest if I gave him a hot shower in exchange," I explained. "I warned him my mother wouldn't let a ghost into the house, but he ignored me."

"Ah," she said. "Yeah, I could have warned you about that weird obsession of his. Also, we'd have had a hotel room with its own shower if your brother hadn't put us in the holding cells."

"You'll both be in there a lot longer if you keep sneaking out whenever his back is turned."

"If Mart hadn't sneaked out, he wouldn't have found your summoning spell," she said. "I told you there'd be evidence hidden in here somewhere."

"Where is he now?"

"He offered to distract the police."

Oh boy. "Then I hope you came here to help me figure out *what* the summoning spell was used for."

"Depends where it is." She turned away from my dad's cottage. "Show me?"

"It's behind my mother's house, but there're two police officers prowling around there," I told her. "Also, it's just a pile of sage in the bushes. If your brother didn't find anything else, there's nothing more for you to find."

If I stayed with her, I'd land myself in hot water with

Ramsey yet again, but how many more chances would I get to learn about the afterworld and its assorted monsters direct from someone who'd been there herself? Like it or not, I needed Maura's information.

Fine. As she left the cottage behind, I joined her. "If someone used a summoning spell in the forest, why is there no longer a single trace of whatever kind of monster it was used to summon?"

"Who's to say there isn't?" She didn't break her stride, but she did slow down a little so I could keep pace with her. "I assumed it was still in the woods somewhere. It's not like I've had time to look around."

I indicated Tansy, who'd scaled a tree alongside the path. "If there was a monster from the afterworld nearby, the wildlife would avoid the forest. When the Ghast was on the loose, there wasn't a bird to be seen. Even my familiar avoided the forest."

A furrow appeared in her brow. "Are those campers still at the police station?"

"No, they aren't." What did that have to do with anything? "My brother sent them home yesterday. I thought you knew."

She stopped in her tracks. "No. I've been in a holding cell, haven't I?"

"What's the problem?" I gave her a questioning look, but she averted her gaze. "The campers' story indicated that none of them was involved in killing their friend."

She groaned. "Your dad said they lived near the playing field… Where is that?"

"You *were* eavesdropping." But her voice held an unmistakable hint of concern, if not outright panic. "What's the issue?"

"The issue is that those campers might still be in danger." She stood on tiptoe, peering through the trees. "The playing field is somewhere near here, isn't it?"

"Yes." I indicated the path to the left, winding away from my dad's house. "If you want to pay a visit to the campers, please don't freak them out by using your shadowy power on them again."

"Believe it or not, I don't usually do that kind of thing in front of witnesses," she replied. "It wasn't me who attacked their campsite. It's the truth."

I'd have to take her word for it, because if they really were in danger, Maura would be better equipped to warn them. Not least because I didn't know *what* I was supposed to warn them about.

I led the way to the field which Harvey's team used for practise. They must have finished early, because there were no broomsticks in the air that I could see, and when we skirted the field, Maura came to an abrupt halt.

"Oh no."

"What?" I followed her gaze and saw the body lying across a fork in the path. "Oh no."

Even before we got close to his body, I recognised him as one of the badger shifters from the campsite, the red-haired one who'd been talking to Ralph. Unlike his unfortunate friend, he did at least have his clothes on, but as with the first victim, there wasn't a mark on him. Nothing to indicate what had caused his death.

My gaze snapped up to Maura. "You don't look surprised. Did you know he was going to die?"

"Not him specifically, but I hazarded a guess that another of the campers would be next."

"Based on what?" I folded my arms across my chest. "Tell me the truth. Who—or what—killed him?"

She sucked in a breath. "A beast from the afterworld, but not one you're likely to be familiar with."

"All right." Having had enough of her evasiveness, I reached for my phone and called Ramsey's number.

To my surprise, he answered right away. "What is it, Robin? Let me guess—you've 'found' my missing prisoner?"

"Ah…"

Wait, he wouldn't accuse Maura of committing the crime, would he? Come to think of it, she'd certainly had time to murder the shifter before she came to my dad's cottage, given her ability to walk through the shadows, but why would she then lead me directly to the body?

"No. One of the three surviving campers is dead. I found the body near the practise field."

He swore. "Wait for me there."

"Hang on—"

He ended the call before I could finish my sentence. Maura had moved and now stood with her head bent over the body as if looking for clues. "He's coming here?"

"You're not going to pull another disappearing act, are you?"

"I'm considering it."

At least I knew where I stood. "This doesn't look good for you, you know. If you knew he was going to die, why not warn me beforehand?"

"You think your brother is going to blame me for his death?" she guessed. "Despite the evidence that someone else used a summoning spell?"

"You said yourself that you have no need of any props to summon a monster from the afterworld."

A breeze swept in as she straightened upright, whether an effect of her Reaper powers or a coincidence of the weather, I didn't know.

"If you aren't going to tell my brother why you're here, you can tell *me* the truth. You owe me."

"I told you, I was in the area looking for a ghost…"

When I made to interrupt, she added, "All right, the ghost was a dead end. I was going to leave, but I sensed someone using a summoning spell elsewhere in the forest. Reapers are more tuned in to the afterworld than regular people are. I didn't know *where* the spell was used, but I followed the trail."

"And stumbled upon our town?"

I looked to the bushes, hearing rustling, but it was just Tansy. My familiar crouched under the bush, her fluffy tail trembling.

"Tansy, can you sense the monster?"

"No, but it's creepy," she said. "And cold."

"But… Harvey's team was on the practise field earlier this afternoon." My blood chilled. He'd had a lucky escape—and so had my dad, for that matter. "Shifters come here all the time. How can the monster have been this close to the town without anyone noticing?"

Maura opened her mouth to reply and then closed it when her ghostly brother came zooming over to us.

"Ooh, you found another dead body."

"I'm aware of that, Mart," Maura said. "This is a problem."

"Yes, it certainly is." My brother came sprinting over to join us, and his eyes bulged at the sight of Maura. "Returned to the scene of the crime, did you?"

Maura grimaced. "This isn't my work. Your sister told you about the summoning spell, didn't she?"

"I did," I interjected. "And Maura was just telling me what kind of monster we're dealing with. It's invisible, right?"

"Is it a ghost?" Tansy piped up, emerging from under the bushes.

Maura's shoulders slumped. "It's not invisible. Not exactly…"

"Then what is it?" I looked to her brother and repeated Tansy's question. "A ghost?"

"No," she said. "I mean, it *is*, but demons are… They aren't like regular spirits."

Demons. Weren't they the most dangerous creatures in the afterworld?

"Demons?" Ramsey's voice carried a dangerous edge. "I don't see a mark on the body."

"The highest level of demons kill their prey without leaving any physical signs," Maura said in a distasteful tone. "They possess a person and drain the life out of them. Literally. We're looking at a class three demon at the very least—"

"There is no 'we,'" Ramsey said. "You've used up your last chance with this latest stunt—and Robin, you should have brought her back to jail right away."

"I'm aware of that, but the dead body kind of took precedence." I reached down to let Tansy scamper up my arm, where she perched on my shoulder with her tail wrapped comfortingly around my neck. "Aren't you more concerned about the demon? Where is it now, Maura?"

"At a guess, it's possessing someone else," she said. "They tend to move between hosts."

"That's why it left no footprints except human ones." I shivered. "Is there any way to identify who it's possessing?"

"Yes," Maura said, "but if the police let this guy walk free without noticing he had an inhuman hitchhiker, it's safe to say you're all in over your heads."

"That's quite enough," Ramsey said through clenched teeth. "You *and* your brother are going back to the holding cells."

"Hang on," I said. "Do you think locking up the one person who might know where the demon is hiding is the best idea?"

"She has no proof to back up her claims," he said, "and she's hardly the only person who knows what a demon is."

"Do you know how to *banish* a demon?" Maura challenged. "How many more people might die before you can find it?"

"She has a point," I said to Ramsey.

"What about me?" Mart said. "You can't make me get back in a cell. Your sister promised me a hot shower."

"A *what*?" Ramsey shot me an accusing stare. "What did you do?"

"I didn't do anything," I said. "He decided I owed him a favour in exchange for finding the site of the summoning spell."

"You'd never have found it without me," Mart said smugly. "I helped your investigation. You're welcome."

Luckily for all of us, it was at that moment that Seth and Shana came running into view. Evidently, my brother had called and warned them while he was on his way to the forest.

"You found the runaway prisoners?" Seth asked, while Shana's eyes widened at the sight of the shifter's body.

"Yes," said Ramsey. "Can you escort them back to the jail at once?"

"Can we please skip the part where you disbelieve me and lock me up again?" Maura sighed as Seth approached with a pair of handcuffs at the ready. "I know I shouldn't have left the jail, but why would I help Robin find the shifter's body if I was the one who put it there? If I'd summoned that demon, I'd have been lying low, not wandering the forest."

Ramsey's stubborn expression didn't budge, but I wished there was something I could say to convince him to make an exception to his usual stringent rules. The police had never dealt with a demon before, and if it was possessing someone else right this instant, how long would it be until it killed again?

"How long does a demon generally possess a host for?" I asked Maura.

"Until they die," she said. "Or the demon gets bored and has enough power stored up to switch hosts. Also, they're very good at hiding, so it's not as simple as lining people up and asking if they're possessed."

"How are we to know you're not possessed yourself?" Ramsey queried.

"Reapers are immune. Look it up."

She didn't say another word as the officers hauled her away. A sinking feeling in my chest told me that it might already be too late for whoever the demon had chosen as its next host. Whoever it was.

The monster wasn't loose in the forest, but the truth was worse. It was inside Wildwood Heath itself.

9

Maura might be on her way back to the holding cells, but there was no way to contain her brother. He remained at the scene, looking entirely too cheerful for someone standing next to a corpse. Or rather, floating. His feet skimmed the ground, a breeze stirring my hair, and he grinned cheekily at us.

"You can try putting handcuffs on me if you like," he said to my brother. "It'd be funny."

"Don't try me," said Ramsey, who looked as if he wished he'd volunteered to take Maura back to prison himself instead of staying behind with her troublesome ghostly brother. "I realise you aren't bound by mortal constraints, but—"

"Not bound by mortal constraints," he repeated. "That's a nice way of saying 'dead.' I'm stealing it."

Ramsey's scowl deepened. "You should know, I carry sage in my pockets."

"Ooh, I'm terrified." Mart lifted his hands, and a gust of air ruffled my hair.

From what I'd seen of his ghostly powers so far, he might

be able to give Grandma a run for her money, which was mildly worrying to contemplate. If this level of mobility was what we could expect from her in future, I might have to ask Maura to perform an exorcism after all. Assuming she didn't end up in jail indefinitely.

Ramsey turned his accusing stare onto me instead. "Why exactly did you make a deal with this ghost?"

"It wasn't intentional," I said. "He'd already escaped jail—"

"With your familiar's help."

Tansy ducked her head behind my neck, and I sighed.

"Not my idea. You must have realised keeping a ghost locked up was an exercise in futility," I said.

"It wasn't intended to be permanent." He studied the shifter's body and furrowed his brow. "The most likely culprit who summoned this supposed demon is a Reaper. You don't lose your abilities when you die, is that correct?"

Mart looked affronted. "*I* certainly didn't summon any demons. I find them to be incredibly dull conversationalists."

"You know about them, though," I ventured. "Same as your sister. Demons are—what? Overpowered ghosts that can possess people?"

"They used to be human?" Even Ramsey looked curiously at Mart; I assumed his desire to know more about the enemy had temporarily outweighed his need to maintain control. "Is that right?"

"Once," said Mart, with a distasteful expression on his face. "A while ago. They don't have any traces of humanity left, which makes them rather bland, in my opinion."

"You've had a lot of experience with demons, have you?" Ramsey said.

Mart turned his back. "I'm not answering any questions until your sister keeps her word."

"You want to hear what he has to say, don't you?" I asked

Ramsey. "He only takes payment in the form of hot showers, but we can arrange that, can't we?"

"That's more like it." Mart spun back around, a grin on his face. "You *do* need to hear what I have to say. If you don't want to listen to my sister, I'm the best option. The better option, in fact."

Ramsey scowled. "I am *not* paying for a hotel room for a ghost."

I bit back a laugh. It was no surprise that Ramsey wouldn't be a fan of that idea, but without Maura or her brother's help, I wouldn't even know how to go about *finding* the demon's current host, let alone evicting it without the unfortunate person ending up dead.

The shifter's body caught my gaze again, and my brief amusement slipped away. "Ramsey, Dad's house isn't far from here. The Sky Hopper team was using the field for practise a few hours ago too."

"What's your point?"

"My point is that the demon might easily have possessed any of them." An involuntary tremor entered my voice. "We need to stop it, even if it means requesting the help of someone you'd otherwise rather avoid working with."

"She's right," Mart said. "I'm willing to bet my sister is the only living person in this entire town who can't be possessed."

"Convenient."

"Ramsey." I made to catch his arm, but he shook me off.

Ramsey paced down the path, where several other officers were approaching. At a guess, they'd come to remove the body and seal off the scene, but as long as the person the demon possessed remained at large, the whole *town* was a potential crime scene.

While my brother talked to the officers, I approached Mart. "If someone's possessed, is there any way to tell from the outside? I mean, do they start speaking in tongues or something?"

"Most demons are smarter than that," he replied. "You'll have to ask my sister the rest. Or keep your word."

"Why would they kill people, though?" Tansy piped up from behind my ear. "If they're possessing someone, wouldn't they want to blend in?"

"What's your familiar squeaking about?" Mart said. "I can't understand a word she says."

"She wants to know why the demon would kill their host if they're dependent upon being disguised as a human to keep hidden."

"They feed on life energy," he said. "It's what enables them to stay in this realm instead of being dragged back to the afterworld. Eventually they run out of juice, and if nobody else is available…"

"Delightful." I dropped my voice when the officers looked in our direction. "Can someone be possessed and not know it?"

"Yes, and that's enough questions. You still owe me a shower."

He had a one-track mind. Not that that was unusual for a ghost, but I would need to convince my brother first. As Ramsey made to leave the scene with one of his officers, I moved to follow them.

"The person who's currently possessed must have been here recently," I murmured to Tansy. "Maybe we can find witnesses."

"There's no wildlife to ask," Tansy pointed out. "I bet it was one of those campers, though. There are only two left."

"There is that." I hoped the same had occurred to Ramsey.

As I moved behind the officer leaving the scene, Mart went whizzing past me and blew onto the back of my brother's neck.

"Hey—do you *want* to get locked up again?" I hissed at him.

Mart zoomed back to my side. "They still haven't learned it's pointless to cage a Reaper."

"Yeah, but I don't think locking up your sister when there's a demon on the loose is going to do anything but embolden it to claim another victim," I said. "Assuming it even knows there's a Reaper in town."

How intelligent were demons? More so than ghosts, I guessed, but I had entirely too little information to make an educated guess on how to deal with the demon myself. Without employing our disgraced Reaper.

"It might not know she's here," Mart said. "The police have ensured she's never got near enough to make eye contact with the demon, so they have that going for them, I suppose."

"Are you sure? She and the campers were at the police station at the same time."

"There is that."

If one of the campers had been possessed at that moment, my brother and the other officers had had a close call. *How can I talk him into letting her go? Especially when she isn't exactly helping to prove her own innocence?*

"Tansy," I whispered, "what d'you think would convince him to let her go?"

"I'd have thought another murder would be enough," she said, "but apparently not."

"He doesn't actually think Maura killed that guy, surely." Though it was beyond me to tell how much of Ramsey's actions were due to suspicion and how much was simple stubbornness. "Mart—is there a limit to your sister's shadowy powers? I mean, could she have walked from the jail to the crime scene and killed someone without the police noticing?"

"Theoretically, yes, but I won't let you trick me into answering any more questions."

"Don't you want to help argue in your sister's favour?" I asked. "If she's let out of jail, you can rent a room at the local inn. Then you'll be able to have all the showers you like."

"Argue in her favour?" He snorted. "Your brother won't even listen to you, and you're supposed to be Head Witch, aren't you?"

"Oi." He was right, but Ramsey would always pick the law over self-preservation. I'd have to appeal to the part of my brother that had no desire to let any of our family members fall victim to the demon if I wanted to convince him to let Maura go.

Whatever he might claim, Mart continued to tail me all the way from the woodland path to the police station.

Upon reaching the doors, Ramsey caught my eye. "I assume you didn't bring Maura's brother with you so I can lock him up too?"

"No, he's… I'm not sure *why* he's here, to be honest."

"To hold your sister to her word," Mart answered. "And to annoy you."

Ramsey narrowed his eyes at the ghost. "I'm going to interrogate *your* sister, and I'll thank you not to interrupt this time."

"I didn't know you were going to question her again." I followed him into the lobby. "Ramsey, we know the demon is almost certainly possessing someone else in town, and the only witness who might be able to tell us its location is dead. If Maura is right about how they feed on human life energy, how long before another victim is claimed?"

"A day." Maura's answer drifted out from behind an open door to one of the questioning rooms. "Give or take."

"It's true." Mart zipped across the lobby, causing a stack of papers to fall off the receptionist's desk.

As Julian scrambled to pick them up, I seized the chance to approach the room in which Maura waited to be questioned.

Ramsey caught my shoulder from behind. "Robin, I did *not* give you permission to sit in on this questioning. Or your familiar."

"Hello again." Maura tried to angle her chair towards the door so she could look at us properly, but with her hands cuffed to the table, it was somewhat difficult for her to move. "Look, I'm trying to help you out. Demons feed on human life force and take a victim every few days, so you have a bit of leeway, but not much."

"What makes you think we need your help?"

"Ramsey, think about it," I said in a low voice. "When a demon possesses someone, they can walk around in public without anyone being any the wiser. Except a Reaper."

"I beg to differ," Ramsey said. "If you're correct and one of the two surviving campers is possessed, I have every intention of bringing them back here to the police station for further questioning. If one of them does turn out to be possessed, we can keep them contained with relative ease."

"Oh." Not a bad idea, but I didn't for a minute believe that keeping a demon contained would be that easy. "There's no telling what the demon might do when you have it cornered, though. What if it attacks your officers? And how would you get the demon out of the camper's body without it killing the host?"

"I know how," Maura said from behind the door. "Granted, they're usually pretty reluctant to let go of their host, but if you're careful, you might be able to pull it off. If you're willing to risk the host's life, that is."

Ramsey glared at her through the open door. "You might go by different rules in your own home, Reaper, but you're a visitor here, and I have no reason to take your advice over our own experts'."

"I thought I was a suspect," she said. "Not a visitor."

Ramsey ignored her, beckoning me to follow him into his office. "Robin, a word, please."

"Fine." I entered the office. Prickles sat on my brother's desk in front of the printed photos from earlier, while Tansy jumped off my shoulder to perch on top of a filing cabinet. "What is it?"

"Robin, my officers are already speculating on whether you were involved in setting Maura and her brother free from the holding cells," he said. "More than once, in fact."

"I didn't break her out of jail—either time," I added. "She showed up in the forest when I was already there."

"Your familiar helped her brother escape, Maura," he said. "I don't appreciate being undermined by my own sister."

"He's a ghost. Imprisoning him was dubious from the start." I glanced at Tansy, who hid behind her fluffy tail. "Fine, I'm sorry I went behind your back. I just feel like you should be treating the fact that someone in town is possessed as a more serious issue than Maura disrespecting you. I don't want anyone else to get killed."

"It's not the disrespect that concerns me," he said in a low voice. "She *is* a suspect, and believe it or not, my officers and I have a contingency plan set up in case of another attack from the afterworld. We don't need her help."

"Then why are you questioning her again?"

"Because I want to find out what she knows," he said. "Without having to make any absurd promises to ghosts."

"I take issue with that." Mart floated through the office door with a gust of wind that knocked several papers off the desk. "Maybe it's you who needs to learn respect."

"He did help me find the evidence." I picked up the papers Mart had dislodged and handed them to a disgruntled Prickles. "And Maura already told me the truth about how she found our town. She sensed someone using a summoning spell from the other side of the forest and came directly here without knowing what she'd find. Everything else, she's figured out as she went along."

"Including that there was a demon here?" Ramsey slammed a hand on top of the papers to stop Mart knocking them over again. "How long has she known, exactly? If she's been aware of its presence here from the start, she's a liability who hid the truth from the police at the cost of at least one life."

That I couldn't deny. "Yeah. I know. But I'm not seeing many options here if we want to get rid of that demon without anyone else dying. Don't forget it took several sceptres to banish the last monster, and unless you have one of those lying around the office—"

"You're saying *you* want to banish the demon?"

"If you won't let Maura try, yes." I gave him a hard stare. "Especially if I'm the target."

"That won't be necessary," he said. "I did say I was going to bring in the surviving campers again, didn't I?"

"I don't think cornering the demon here at the police station is going to help," I said. "Not with one Reaper handcuffed to a table and the other a ghost."

At my words, Mart blew a raspberry at me and flew out of the room again.

"The demon can't kill more than once in a day." Ramsey made for the door himself. "I *have* researched the subject, and I intend to learn more from the Reaper myself, if you'll let me."

"That gives you what, twenty-four hours?" I took a step back as he pushed open the office door. "Ramsey—"

He brushed me off, walking from his office to the room in which Maura sat. *Screw it.* I entered behind him, and while he didn't look thrilled, he didn't tell me to leave either. As I joined him on the other side of the table, I crossed my fingers behind my back that Maura was at least vaguely cooperative. For everyone's sakes.

"I didn't summon the demon," Maura began. "Just to make one thing clear up front."

"Then how did you know it was here?" Ramsey said. "I understand that you told my sister that you sensed the summoning spell from the other side of the forest, but I'd rather hear the account from you myself."

"My Reaper abilities let me sense every time someone nearby uses a spell that involves the afterworld," she said. "I didn't know they'd summoned a demon at the time, but the spell was strong enough that I sensed it from miles outside of your town. I figured it was worth following the trail."

"Did you get here before or after the camper died?"

"After," she replied. "I don't expect you to believe me, but if the demon had been around when I arrived, I'd have been able to find it. Also, if I'd summoned it myself, I wouldn't have needed to use a spell."

"That's true." Mart drifted through the door to join her. "In fact, you can ask any ghost in town if they sensed the spell and they'd be able to tell you."

"Really?" Might Grandma have noticed? I hadn't thought of asking her, but I also hadn't seen her since her impromptu excursion.

"Don't change the subject," Ramsey said. "You lied when you said you were here looking for a ghost, correct?"

"No, that's why I was originally visiting a town over on the other side of the woods," she said. "Also, I was telling the truth when I said I didn't know people lived *in* the forest. Your town is well-hidden."

"For good reason," Ramsey said. "Assuming you're being

truthful, why did you stay in Wildwood Heath after you realised your mistake?"

"To get rid of the demon, I told you," Maura said. "After it's gone, I'll gladly go home. I have people who'll be wondering where I am."

"One of whom is the head of the police in Hawkwood Hollow," Ramsey said. "Yes, I looked you up."

"Good for you," Maura said. "If you checked, you'll know I work at the Riverside Inn and hunt ghosts in my spare time."

"You also aren't a registered Reaper."

"Because I'm not actively working as one. I went through all this with my region's Reapers already. They don't care."

"I find that hard to believe," said Ramsey. "If I let you go, can I trust you not to get in my way?"

"You can't," she said. "In fact, I'm pretty much guaranteed to get in your way if I keep trying to find this demon, but I'm also the only person here who might be able to send it back where it belongs without anyone else getting killed, so I'd say it's worth the trade-off."

"That's not for you to decide," said Ramsey. "You don't know who summoned it? Is that the truth?"

"Yes, it is," she said. "That's *your* job, not mine. I only care about dealing with the demon."

That ought to pacify my brother, though he retained an expression that reminded me of the time I tried to convince him to wade into the sea when we were kids. Even at eight, he'd hated the idea of getting his feet covered in wet sand.

"And you'll be able to tell on sight if either of the campers is possessed?" he asked.

"Yeah, I will," she said. "You might be able to figure it out too. If the demon wants to show itself, the person's eyes will turn completely black. You can't mistake it. Unfortunately, they're also good at hiding, especially the strong ones, so you're going to need my help."

"We'll see," he said. "You can deal with the demon however you see fit, but leave the matter of arresting the culprit to the police."

"I'd be glad to," she said. "We understand one another, then."

They glared at one another, and then Ramsey grudgingly removed her handcuffs. "One sign of trouble and these go back on. That clear?"

"Crystal." She stretched out her hands. "Let's find that demon."

10

With Maura no longer behind bars, it ought to have been easy to plan our next move, but Ramsey refused to let her act alone. While he waited for the campers to show up, he insisted that she remain in the police station. I stayed put, too, glad I'd had the presence of mind to grab my sceptre earlier.

"If one of them was possessed, we'd know right away, wouldn't we?" I asked Maura. "I mean, even without your Reaper powers, their reaction to the news that another of their friends died ought to give away if one of them is possessed by an unfeeling monster."

"You aren't wrong," Maura said, "but demons can be crafty, and sometimes the host doesn't even know they're present. If you question the campers carefully, you might be able to pick out if they have any gaps in their memories, but you'd be surprised how easy it is for demons to blend in. They've had a lot of practise."

"That's enough," Ramsey said, as Mart knocked another stack of papers off the top of a filing cabinet. "Robin, take the Reaper with you to the nearest inn and help her check in."

"You want me to babysit?"

I raised a brow at Maura, who if anything was more competent than half the staff here. Certainly more so than the receptionist, who tripped over his own seat as he rushed to gather the papers Mart had knocked onto the floor.

"Are you sure the campers won't get here while we're gone?"

"I'll let you know if they show up." He made a sweeping gesture at the door. "And take the Reaper's brother with you too."

"You did promise him a shower." Maura sauntered towards the door. "You're welcome."

And that was how I ended up helping the confused receptionist at the Owl's Nest Inn check Maura and Mart into separate rooms. Conveying Mart's bizarre request for hot showers to a wizard who couldn't see ghosts was amusing enough, but I couldn't help glancing over at the door every few seconds to see if the two surviving campers had reached the high street yet.

Maura appeared unconcerned. She took the keys from the receptionist and made for the stairs to the upper floor.

"You're going to your room?" I asked.

"Of course I am," she said. "I've been sitting in a cell all day and night. I want a shower."

"And me," Mart said over his shoulder as he drifted upstairs.

"Can I get you anything else, Head Witch?" asked the inn's owner, who kept glancing at my sceptre in awe.

"No—it's fine."

I left the inn and met my familiar outside. "Pretty sure the staff think I have a screw loose, renting a room for a ghost, but I guess they don't want to say no to the Head Witch."

"They gave him his own room?" Tansy lifted her head and then stiffened. "I hope Maura doesn't take too long. Look."

She pointed with her tail as four people walked into view —or rather, three people and one badger. The badger was in the arms of a grim-faced officer, while Seth escorted the other camper—Ralph—towards the police station.

"Can you tell if either of them is possessed?" I asked Tansy as she hopped onto my shoulder.

"No, everything stinks of badger." She wrinkled her nose. "Can demons possess shifters when they're in their animal form?"

"Good question." I'd have to ask Maura when she emerged from her room.

In the meantime, I headed back to the police station, where Ramsey watched the officers escort the two surviving campers across the lobby to the questioning rooms.

"I thought you were watching Maura," he said, with no small level of annoyance. "If she runs off—"

"She won't. You're the one who let her go." I indicated the two campers. "Besides, you can't expect me to ignore that you might have brought a demon in here."

"Keep it down." He strode to the questioning room, in which the officer carrying the badger was attempting to wrestle his captive into a chair.

As I reached the room, Seth moved in to help the other officer and promptly dropped the badger onto the chair.

"Ouch! He bit me," Seth said.

The badger hid underneath the table, while Ralph slumped into the other chair. "Is Cody really dead?"

"He is." Ramsey waited for the other officers to leave the room before attempting to take control of the situation. "When did you last see him?"

"Yesterday," Ralph replied. "After we went home from the police station."

"That's not true." The voice came from underneath the

table, where the second shifter had turned from a badger into a human again. "We saw him earlier, remember?"

"You did?" I walked into the room and addressed the second camper, who was hunched under the table, naked and shivering. "When?"

"We met up at Ralph's house this morning," he said tremulously. "To discuss Phil's death, and—and what to do for his funeral."

"Is that true?" Ramsey asked Ralph, who remained slumped in his seat.

"No," grunted Ralph. "I haven't a clue what Derren's talking about."

"One of you must be telling the truth." With a shiver of unease, I recalled that Maura had mentioned that people who were possessed by demons often had gaps in their memories. "What time did you meet up?"

"Noon, or thereabouts," Ralph said. "Then we all went home."

Hmm. "Including Cody? Is there a reason he might have been walking alone near the field?"

"We live there," Ralph said defensively. "What killed him? It wasn't a human, was it?"

Ramsey gave me a warning look that I couldn't decipher. Did he not want me to mention the demon? I didn't see any signs that either of the teenagers was playing host to a disembodied monster, but given the strong smell of sage drifting in from the lobby, the police had already prepared for the possibility of an attack.

"A person was responsible," I said instead. "Which is why my brother wanted to question you again. Right, Ramsey?"

"Why would we kill our own friends?" Ralph said indignantly. "Who's that weird woman who keeps talking to herself, anyway? The one who you brought here earlier? Is she helping the police?"

"None of your concern," Ramsey said. "Two of your friends died in suspicious circumstances, and we have reason to believe someone has been dabbling in illegal magic that led to their deaths."

"Magic?" the shifter under the table said, his voice a high squeak. "Who? What?"

Ramsey beckoned me to join him near the door, where he addressed me in a low voice. "One of them is lying, possibly both. We need your Reaper friend to determine who it is."

"You want her to come back?" If either of them was possessed, Ralph was the more obvious candidate. I didn't know whether a demon could possess someone who was in the form of a badger, and he was the one who seemed to have gaps in his memories, but I'd prefer Maura to be here when we brought up the subject. "I'll see if she's ready."

I didn't much like the idea of leaving my brother in the same room as a demon, but I didn't see anyone else volunteering to fetch Maura. Inside the lobby, the receptionist was sprinkling sage all over his desk—that would explain the smell—while Seth sat in a nearby chair as he wrapped a bandage around the arm the badger shifter had bitten.

"That thing has a nasty bite," he remarked as I passed. "Where're you going?"

"To find Maura."

I shivered as Tansy's fluffy tail brushed my ear. "You'd think the smell of sage would drag the demon out of hiding."

"Maybe it already did." She hid herself behind my hair. "It's creepy in here."

"Please don't say that." I speed-walked through the automatic doors and veered in the direction of the inn. "Maura said people who are possessed sometimes experience memory loss, which would explain why the shifters' accounts are contradictory. That all but proves Ralph is possessed. I should have asked my brother to handcuff him to the chair."

"That might have provoked it." Tansy jumped off my shoulder as we neared the Owl's Nest Inn. "I'll get her."

"Cheers."

I watched Tansy run up the drainpipe at the side of the inn, and someone inside one of the rooms let out a shriek. Oops. I hoped Tansy hadn't got the wrong room, but it was too late to call her back, so I entered the lobby.

Maura was already downstairs, looking much more refreshed than the last time I'd seen her. "Let me guess… Your brother wants my expertise."

I looked up when another shriek came from above. "I think my familiar might have got into the wrong room."

"No, that's my brother's fault," she said. "He flooded the entire floor."

Oh no. "See why I didn't want him in my mother's house?"

"I'm used to it." She shrugged and followed me out of the inn. "Are both the campers at the police station?"

"One of them may or may not be in the form of a badger, but yes, they are." I paused outside to wait for my familiar.

"And none of them has shown signs of being possessed?"

"No black eyes or anything, but there's some memory loss, I think." I watched a slightly damp Tansy climb down from the drainpipe and shake herself, spraying me with droplets of water. "They both have contradictory accounts of whether they saw the victim today or not. One says they did, the other says they didn't."

"Does your brother expect me to frighten the demon into letting go of its host by unleashing my Reaper powers?" She strode alongside me, heading for the police station. "Or does he think the demon will let go of its host if he asks nicely?"

"Probably the latter." I reluctantly let Tansy climb up my arm and swipe her wet tail over my neck. "The receptionist is piling sage all over the lobby. Might that frighten the demon out?"

"Not unless the host stepped directly into it," she replied. "But most people can't see demons, so if it released its host and bolted, there's no guarantee they'd be able to catch the demon before it possessed someone else."

"How do you normally deal with this kind of thing?"

"Me?" she said. "There is no 'normally.' I don't tend to run into demons every week, but if I were your brother, I'd enclose the suspect in a circle of sage and then try to trick or scare the demon into letting them go. If you're lucky, the person it's possessing won't die in the process, but I can't make any guarantees."

That didn't sound promising, but we were out of other options. When we crossed the police station's lobby to the questioning room, Ramsey waited for Maura.

"Reaper, I want you to identify if either of these two individuals is possessed by a demon."

I wondered if she'd react to his carefully polite tone with a sarcastic comment, but she entered the room without responding.

Inside, the second shifter—Derren, his friend had called him—sat in a chair instead of hiding under a table, and someone had given him a coat to wrap around himself.

"Can demons possess a shifter while they're in animal form?" I whispered to Maura, earning a headshake in response. "Then it's got to be Ralph."

Ralph himself eyed Maura in apparent confusion. "Who are you?"

"Maura." She narrowed her eyes at him. "I'm told you can't remember the last time you saw your friend alive."

"I can," he insisted. "Yesterday."

"This morning," Derren countered. "You must remember."

"I really don't."

Maura was silent for a moment. As she surveyed Ralph, her eyes gained a strange intensity that made me want to back away, and I could have sworn the shadows at her feet darkened and thickened. "How long is the gap in your memories?"

"Who said anything about a gap?" Ralph said defensively.

"You don't remember this morning, right?"

"I do remember," he said. "I was up late last night, and I slept half the day. I didn't see Cody."

"Yes, you did," Derren retaliated.

"We've already been through this." Ramsey waited for us to leave the room. "Maura—I thought you were able to tell if someone was possessed."

"I'm not getting that vibe from him, but there are too many people in here for me to use my Reaper powers," she replied. "The whole place smells of sage too."

"She says the demon would be more likely to come out if she trapped the host in a circle of sage," I whispered to my brother as he closed the door on the suspects. "If you put it around the outskirts of the room…"

"Good luck doing that without the demon noticing," Maura interjected. "Also, that poor guy's friend would get caught in the trap too."

"I see," Ramsey said. "In that case, we'll take it from here."

I blinked in surprise, but Maura gave another casual shrug.

"If you're sure," she said.

"Ramsey." I caught his arm before he could open the door to the questioning room again. "Whatever happened to accepting her help?"

"She said the demon isn't possessing either of the campers."

"That really isn't what she said." My heart sank when Maura strode across the lobby, pausing only to cast a disdainful snort in the direction of Julian's sage-covered desk before she left. "She can banish the demon."

"So can I, but it isn't here," he said. "I'll put the two suspects in the holding cells as a precaution and enclose them in sage to keep them contained."

That was one way to force the demon out, I supposed, but if it wasn't possessing either of them, where was it? If anyone else had interacted with Cody around the time of his death, there were no witnesses to ask.

Unless… "How about I ask Maura to call back Cody's ghost to ask him if he remembers his death?"

I was proud of that idea, but Ramsey was unimpressed.

"Ghosts are hardly reliable."

"Doesn't look like the living people are much better." I was fighting a losing battle on that one, I knew, so I hurried to catch Maura on her way back to the inn.

She slowed her pace a little when she saw me. "Your brother needs to decide if he needs my help or not. He's giving me whiplash."

"I think he expected you to draw out the demon right away," I said. "Ah—is it possible for you to summon Cody's ghost?"

"Who, the newest victim?" she asked. "There's a delay of a couple of days between someone's death and my ability to bring them back. And that's assuming the demon left anything of him to question. They feed on the life force of a person, like I said."

"Creepy." I gave a shudder, glancing back towards the police station. "What did you plan to do tonight? Would you be able to sense the demon's appearance from your room at the inn?"

"Depends how close it is," she said. "I don't think either of those two prisoners is possessed, which means the demon is most likely elsewhere in town."

Maura was the expert, so I had to assume she was right. "I guess it's lying low, but it might try to feed on someone else tomorrow."

"Exactly," she said. "There's nothing we can do at the moment, so once I've dealt with the mess my brother made at the inn, I plan to find a pub and get a decent meal."

"I know a place." I pulled out my phone to text Piper. I didn't know if she'd want to go to dinner with a Reaper, but I needed to make it up to her after our misunderstanding earlier, and Rowan would be finishing her shift soon too. "I can introduce you to some of the locals."

An hour later, the four of us were at the Fox's Den—well, five, counting Mart, who showed no remorse at having flooded the room next to Maura's. I'd had to apply my sceptre to clean up the mess, and while Mum would not be impressed if she found out I'd used my sceptre for such trivial purposes, I was pretty sure she'd have preferred that to me letting him shower in her house.

"I can't believe you met a Reaper." Piper stared at Maura in awe from across the table in the pub.

I'd sat next to Maura to spare the others, and Piper and Rowan had turned to one another for moral support in the face of our new guests.

"Two," Mart added from behind Maura's seat.

"You're a Reaper too?" Rowan asked him.

"Being a ghost doesn't mean I don't have any talents," he said self-importantly.

"No offence intended," she said. "My grandmother is a ghost too."

I gave her a warning look, and she cringed, realising I hadn't wanted her to mention that. In fairness, I hadn't told her not to, but I knew Mum wouldn't want Maura going near the office. Piper, the only one of our group who couldn't see Mart, simply looked confused.

Luckily, the food arrived on the table at that moment, so I seized on the chance to change the subject. "Did you say your boyfriend was the head of your local police force, Maura?"

She picked up her fork. "Yeah, which is why I know how annoyed they get when ghosts or demons are involved in a case. Most of them can't see spirits."

Hmm. "Your boyfriend isn't a wizard?"

"Shifter," she replied. "He's open-minded but most of his fellow officers aren't, and we've had a few scuffles."

"My brother can see ghosts. He's just stubborn."

"Yeah, I get that." She shoved a few fries into her mouth. "The police would usually rather arrest a human suspect than admit the culprit is incorporeal."

"You've met demons before?" asked Piper, who was watching Maura eat with evident confusion, as if she'd assumed she lived on nothing but air.

"Not often," Maura said. "They don't like Reapers much."

"I can't imagine why," said Mart, stealing a fry from his sister's plate. Naturally, when he put it in his mouth, it fell straight through his ghostly form and landed on the floor.

"Cut it out." Maura shooed him away. "Anyway, it's up to the police to figure out who summoned that demon, and you'd better hope they do if you want to avoid this kind of thing happening again."

"Reassuring." I didn't miss the alarmed look that Rowan and Piper shared. "Ramsey's good at his job, stubbornness aside."

"I hope you're right," Maura said. "He'll want to prosecute the summoner, whoever it is, but things have a tendency to get out of hand where demons are concerned. It's a real headache when someone commits murder while possessed and the police have to decide if they're guilty or not."

"Can the demon take complete control of the person they possess?" Piper asked tremulously. "Would they remember?"

"Sometimes they remember," Maura said. "They have no control over what the demon makes them do, but it depends on how strong the demon is. Some can fight. It varies."

"You said the demon is a class three," I recalled. "How high do the numbers go?"

"Five, and you won't meet one of those in a small town like this one. They like bigger targets."

Sensing the others' discomfort, I decided to change the subject… But I had one more question first. "Good to know. If that guy *was* possessed, and the demon let him go, did it possess someone else?"

"I'd guess it did," said Maura. "And we have less than a day to find its unfortunate host before it kills again."

11

Despite Maura's ominous proclamation the previous night, no signs of the demon materialised. I showed up to the office the next morning sleepy but without the guilt of another demon-induced death hanging over me.

"Robin?" Chloe waved her hand in front of my face.

I dragged my attention away from the screensaver on my grandmother's old laptop, which depicted the various Eevee evolutions dancing around a field.

"You need to sign this," she said.

"Fine." I yawned, jaw cracking, and scribbled my signature on the papers she offered me. I'd been in the position of Head Witch long enough to be able to do some tasks on autopilot, but I couldn't help wishing there was a spell that could conjure up a clone of myself to stay in the office while I helped Maura hunt for the missing demon.

I handed Chloe the papers, and she returned to her desk, which was far neater than mine. All her paperwork was carefully arranged around the spot where Carmilla, my grandmother's cat, napped in a puddle of sunlight. Grandma herself had yet to materialise, which at least meant I hadn't had to break the news of Maura's presence in town. Not to mention the demon... assuming she hadn't already sensed its arrival.

Chloe, for one, didn't seem concerned about my grandmother's absence. "You remember we have a meeting this afternoon, don't you?"

"Unfortunately, yes." I'd been hoping to drop by the police office beforehand to check whether my brother's investigation had turned up any new evidence yet, but all I knew was that the two campers had spent the night in the holding cells without any demons materialising.

"We have to go through the budgets for the month," Chloe went on. "And... erm, have you decided whether to say anything about the incident over the weekend yet?"

"Isn't that up to my mother?" As coven leader, she held sway over which information was shared with the coven and what was kept quiet. She'd hinted the previous night that I'd have no choice but to reveal both my friendship with the Reaper *and* the demon's presence in town to the rest of the coven before the information reached them through other means.

"I thought you were helping your brother with the investigation," she said. "The culprit hasn't been caught yet, have they?"

"No, but the person who's possessed isn't the same as the person who actually *summoned* the demon in the first place."

She gave a shudder. "Are you going to tell the coven that a demon is behind the two murders?"

"Again, that's up to Mum," I said. "The tricky thing is that the demon might not still be on the loose if Ramsey hadn't locked up the one person who could get rid of it, so she might want to keep that part quiet."

"Who do you mean? The Reaper?"

I grimaced. "Yes, but we're not using that word. Not in front of—"

"What do you mean, *Reaper*?" Grandma appeared above my desk with an expression of pure indignation. "You called one of them to get rid of me?"

"Of course not." I should have guessed she'd been eavesdropping on us. "There's a demon possessing someone here in Wildwood Heath, and the Reaper came to get rid of it before anyone else gets killed. She doesn't even know you're here."

Not strictly true, given what Rowan had let slip at the pub last night, but Maura would have no inclination to banish Grandma to the permanent afterworld. Not that the idea hadn't tempted me once or twice, but it was the demon who concerned me the most, and now that Grandma was here, I needed to ask if she'd sensed its presence.

"That's not acceptable," she said. "Get rid of her at once."

"I can't get rid of her when I need her help," I said. "The demon has killed two people. Did you sense anything weird in the afterworld lately?"

"I haven't been anywhere near the place."

"Grandma, you're *in* the afterworld, right this instant."

"No, I'm in my office."

Honestly. "Have you seen anything weird here, then?"

"Don't be absurd," she said. "Are you trying to get out of work again?"

"The demon was summoned directly behind our *house*," I told her. "You really didn't sense anything?"

"No, otherwise I would have driven off that rogue Reaper myself."

I raised a brow at her. "She's not a rogue. How do you know so much about Reapers, anyway?"

"Whoever said I did?"

Her defensive tone instantly raised my suspicions. "You

said before that you don't have any books on illegal necromancy, but not everything is up to the Reapers. Who do regular people call when they have a demon? Has that ever been an issue before?"

Even if it hadn't, she and Mum were prepared for every worst-case scenario. Even ones that involved illegal magic. When she didn't respond, I asked, "Can a regular person banish a demon? With or without a sceptre?"

"What kind of a ridiculous question is that?" she said. "Obviously. If you can banish a ghost, you can banish a demon."

"I didn't think it was that simple." The Ghast had proven that, if nothing else. "Head Witches aren't immune to possession, are they?"

Instead of answering, she vanished. Into the afterworld, I assumed. *Haven't been near the place indeed.*

"Thanks for the help, Grandma." I turned to Chloe. "What's up with her?"

"Your guess is as a good as mine," she said. "She's scared of the Reaper, and she might be scared of the demon too."

"You'd think she'd want to help me get rid of it. That way, the Reaper will leave town and she can get back to haunting me in peace."

Granted, banishment spells were the only way to get rid of a demon, and there wasn't much Grandma could do other than cheer from the sidelines. Or shout criticism, as she typically did during our magic lessons. Assuming I was exempt today, I returned to work.

When lunchtime rolled around, I left the office in search of an update on the demon situation. As I reached the high street, I spied Maura through the window of Were's My Coffee, sitting at a table with her ghostly brother.

Rowan gave me a strained smile when I walked in, having just laid out three double-shots of espresso on the table in front of Mart, to the evident confusion of the other patrons and staff.

"What?" Mart said when he caught me looking at the three cups on the table in front of him. "I can only taste coffee if it's really strong."

"Right." I shook my head at him and then faced his sister. "I take it there haven't been any new updates?"

"No, but I didn't expect the demon to come waltzing into my hotel room," she said. "That'd be too simple."

I thought back to Grandma's insistence that she hadn't noticed anything weird in the afterworld. "Ah—is it still too early to summon the victims' ghosts?"

"Not the first one," she said, "but if the demon drained his life essence, there won't be much left of him to summon."

"You're ruining my appetite," Mart griped, reaching for one of the espresso shots. He did manage to lift it into the air, but Maura hastily grabbed it before he tipped it into his mouth.

"I'd rather you didn't make another mess," she said. "If you ask me, the Owl's Nest staff will be glad to be rid of us."

I'm not surprised. Rowan watched the floating cup with round eyes, though she wasn't as confused as the nearby patrons who couldn't see Mart's ghostly hands holding the cup.

"That won't happen until we're rid of this demon," I said in a low voice. "Rowan, can I order a latte and sandwich to go? I should head to the police station and see—"

The café door swung open, and my brother walked in. *Okay, maybe not.*

Everyone stopped staring at Mart to gawk at him instead, but Ramsey ignored them all and stopped at our table. "There you are, Reaper. There's been another attack. You're needed."

"Nice to see you too." Despite her light tone, Maura's face was grim as she rose to her feet.

Mart, meanwhile, grabbed for the espresso and missed, causing the cup to tumble to the floor. Coffee splattered Rowan, Maura, and me—not to mention Ramsey, who might have tried to strangle Mart if he hadn't been a ghost.

"This is serious," my brother hissed. "The victim wasn't harmed this time, but one of my officers was attacked. I won't have your antics undermining me."

"Simmer down." Maura sidestepped the table, dripping coffee everywhere. "What do you mean, he wasn't harmed?"

Rowan moved in to clean up the mess, which had also hit everyone at the table next to theirs—including the unfortunate shifter, Dale Longford. If you asked me, he really ought to stop frequenting the café when I was around.

"One of your officers?" I followed Ramsey towards the café door, glad I'd brought my sceptre with me. "Who?"

"Seth. He's in the hospital."

My heart dove into my shoes. "I thought you said he wasn't hurt."

"I won't discuss this here."

Ramsey swept out of the café, while Maura waved her wand to divest her clothing of the spilled coffee. She then did the same to the table, earning a grateful smile from Rowan, who then mouthed *stay safe* at me as I left.

"When did this happen?" I halted when Maura gave another wave of her wand, causing my clothes to instantly dry. "Ah, thanks. Ramsey, how badly is he hurt?"

Ramsey, whose clothes were also dry, didn't offer Maura so much as a word of thanks. "Not seriously, but I asked for visitors to be barred from the ward, just in case the demon comes back."

"It was possessing someone else at the time?" Maura

made an *oh* noise of understanding. "Can't you slow down? I can't help you if I don't know the details."

"One of my officers was attacked." The tightness in Ramsey's voice betrayed his anger. "We found him lying on the ground outside, disorientated, and he said that a man with black eyes attacked him."

"A man with black eyes?" Maura echoed. "He doesn't remember anything else?"

"The attacker hit him from behind, so no," Ramsey said.

"Hit him?" I echoed. "The demon didn't… drain the life from him?"

"No," Maura answered in place of my brother. "They don't usually need to feed on more than one person in a short time frame. Honestly, I did think the first two victims were closer together than I'd have expected."

"Why would it randomly attack someone else, then?" I asked.

"Who knows why demons do anything?" she said. "If Seth can describe his attacker, it would help. Can't I talk to him?"

"I expect he'll be discharged by the evening." Ramsey slowed as we neared the police station. "If you want to come back here to listen to his statement on the attack, I can allow that."

"All right, as long as I don't end up in a cell." Maura followed him in.

I wished I'd brought Tansy with me. I'd left her in the garden at the coven's headquarters, figuring she'd be happier to avoid all demon-related discussions.

"Are those two campers still in here?" I asked Ramsey. "Or did you let them out?"

"They're still in the holding cells." He beckoned both of us inside his office.

As before, Prickles the hedgehog perched on Ramsey's desk next to the photos of the prints in the forest.

"You're back." Prickles's beady eyes assessed Maura.

"I believe it's wise to let the Reaper know the results of the report we received from the coroner who examined the body of the first victim," my brother said. "They ruled out poison, or a curse—any of the common ones, anyway."

"We already knew that," I said. "There aren't physical signs when a demon drains the life from someone, are there?"

"No, which makes this incredibly difficult to explain to the officers who cannot see ghosts themselves," Ramsey said. "More than half of them can't see spirits, and our knowledge is limited enough that I saw fit to consult certain... certain texts we confiscated from others with less scrupulous means of achieving their aims."

"You mean the books you confiscated from the Henbanes?" I'd known he'd brought them to the police station, but I'd assumed he'd sooner sit on Prickles than consult a book on dodgy magic.

A slight flush darkened his cheeks, but he inclined his head. "I flipped through them to learn the details of what we might be facing. According to the texts, demons can enable humans to achieve feats that they wouldn't normally be able to. Seth said the attacker nearly strangled him with his bare hands."

"Yeah... That's a demon," said Maura. "Is there any *new* information, though? Or are you still working on convincing your officers that this is a demon at all?"

"I'm establishing a timeline," he replied. "The demon possessed and killed the first victim and then likely possessed Ralph next, before it moved to his friend and killed him too. That doesn't fit with the books' claims that a demon only needs to feed every two or three days."

"I thought I already told you that," Maura said. "Demons

can switch hosts once per day at most, but this one seems stronger than average."

"Are you sure it's not possessing *Seth* now?" I asked suspiciously. "Why else wouldn't it have finished the job?"

"Studying the behaviour of demons isn't a refined art," Maura said. "It *might* be possessing him. Or not."

"It didn't kill Ralph, either," I added. "He had gaps in his memories, but the demon let him off lightly. Does he remember anything else from yesterday morning?"

"Not that he's been willing to share," said Ramsey, "which is why I refrained from letting him and Derren out of the holding cells."

"You might as well let them go," said Maura. "That other guy shifted into a badger so many times that it would have shaken the demon out. They're not fans of possessing animals."

"I figured as much," I said. "I wonder if that's how Ralph shook it off?"

"He had nothing more to say," said Ramsey. "Neither did his companion."

"What about Tiffany?" I asked. "Have you spoken to her again?"

"No, I certainly have not," said Ramsey. "I have no desire to listen to her gloating."

"But you do think she's involved." I could see Maura watching curiously, but I kept my attention on my brother. "It sounds like those books you confiscated from her coven were comprehensive enough. I wonder how many of her coven members read them before the police confiscated them?"

"Fine."

I blinked. "Fine what?"

"You can talk to Tiffany yourself," he said. "Not you,

Maura. Or your brother either. There's no use in you staying here until Seth is out of the hospital."

"Ramsey, you could stand to be a bit nicer to our guest," I said in a low voice, though Maura herself appeared unbothered at his curt manner.

"Our 'guest' flooded the upstairs floor of the inn and spilled coffee all over the café," he pointed out. "And I notice that we never had trouble with demons *before* she showed up."

"Come on, you don't actually suspect her, do you?" I assumed his abrasiveness was due to his worry on Seth's behalf, which was understandable. The guy was one of the nicer people who worked here. I bloody well *hoped* he wasn't possessed.

Ramsey didn't dignify that with a reply. He did, however, lead me through the door to the holding cells without a fuss.

Inside, the strong smell of sage hit me. Both campers were secured in cells surrounded by heaps of the stuff, and while Ralph appeared to be asleep, Derren was no longer in the form of a badger.

He watched us walk past his cell, his expression grim. "It attacked someone else, didn't it?"

"Yes." I mentally flipped a coin and opted to be honest. "Not fatally this time. Remember anything else?"

"I'm not the one having trouble with his memory." He jerked his head towards Ralph's sleeping form. "I think the demon chewed a hole in his brain."

"Pretty sure that's not a thing." Not that Maura had been allowed to come into the holding cells with me, and Ramsey's disapproving expression suggested he didn't want me talking to the campers either. "He *was* possessed, though. Do you know why the demon let him go? Did he shift into a badger at any point yesterday?"

His brow wrinkled. "Yeah… He did. Why?"

"Enough." My brother steered me through the holding

cells and towards the door leading to the highest security part of the prison.

Conscious that I didn't have much longer before I had to return to work, I entered the dingy corridor where the most dangerous criminals resided and made straight for our resident villainess's cell.

Tiffany sat on a bench that faced the door, one leg crossed over the other, watching the door as if she'd expected a visitor. "Robin. What a surprise."

"Spare me," I said. "You knew I'd come here. You were counting on it, I bet."

"Yes, but I'm surprised you'd come to me for help with your demon."

"I don't need help," I told her. "I need to know who summoned it, and the last incident involving the afterworld had your sticky fingerprints all over it. Who'd you give instructions to?"

Her expression remained impassive. "I admire your faith in my ability to act while incarcerated."

"Hardly. You probably taught half your coven to do it."

"Again, you flatter me. I only teach the best."

My jaw twitched. "You had someone do your dirty work. It's obvious. If you conveniently remember any names, I think the police would appreciate it if you told them."

"I'll take that under advisement."

Meaning she had no intention of giving anything away. "Those books of yours are rare. Mind telling me how you got them?"

"No, I don't think I will."

I lifted the sceptre so that its glow shone into her cell. Her gaze landed on the purple gem, a hint of greed entering her eyes. "Sure about that?"

She laughed. "You can't threaten me, fool. A Head Witch

studying demons isn't so unusual, if you've ever wondered. In fact, I'd wager the apple doesn't fall too far from *that* tree."

"What the hell is that supposed to mean?"

"It means this conversation is over," Ramsey said. "If I find proof of your involvement, Tiffany, I'll have you sent to a secure facility elsewhere."

"That won't make a difference," Tiffany said with a laugh. "As always, it was a pleasure talking to you, Head Witch."

Rattled, I walked away from her cell. When we were out of hearing distance, I turned to my brother. "Did she just insinuate that someone in our family has studied demons?"

"She's a known liar, Robin." He swept ahead and opened the door leading to the regular part of the prison. "Don't you have to go back to work?"

I did, but this was far more important—and urgent. "I'll try to talk Mum into letting me have the afternoon off."

"Good luck with that," he said. "Until Seth is released from the hospital, there's no sense in you staying here."

"What if he *is* possessed?" I asked. "Will you let Maura help?"

"If I say 'yes,' will you get out from under my feet?" He indicated the front doors. "Look, your familiar is there."

You haven't won this one, Ramsey. Or Tiffany.

Tansy stood on her hind legs, trying to get my attention, so I went to join her outside.

"Sorry, I should have brought you with me. There was another attack. Not a fatal one, but I was worried."

"There's trouble back at the office too," she said. "It looks like the entire council is demanding you come back and explain yourself."

Oh boy.

12

I hadn't even had time to grab lunch, but it couldn't be helped. I speed-walked back to the office, Tansy riding on my shoulder. "What's the issue?"

"Aunt Shannon."

I groaned. "Of course she's stuck her broomstick in. She's almost as bad as Tiffany—and trust me, that's saying something."

Tansy's tail wagged. "You didn't speak to *her* again, did you?"

"I wanted to see if she'd admit to being involved in this demon issue," I said. "I'd bet my sceptre she is, but she tried to distract me by insinuating that past Head Witches in my family have studied demons in the past."

"That's ridiculous," Tansy said indignantly. "She was trying to deflect the blame. I guarantee it."

"Yeah."

Upon reaching the street where our coven's headquarters lay, I found Mum waiting in front of the building.

"What's going on?" I asked.

"You have a meeting to attend, Robin."

"I know, but I thought I was allowed to do what I wanted during my breaks." Had the council found out about the demon? "What's Aunt Shannon done?"

Mum didn't answer, and even Tansy looked subdued when I left her sitting outside the door. The meeting room was a familiar-free zone, but I wished I could bring her with me for moral support. Heart in my throat, I made my way through the lobby. The meeting room door was slightly open, revealing a packed table… and Maura sitting among the council members.

Aunt Shannon smirked up at me from her seat on Maura's right-hand side. Had she ambushed Maura as soon as she'd left the police station? It was a miracle her brother hadn't come along for the ride, but the accusing stares from the rest of the council told me that it would be impossible to talk my way out of this one.

Dammit. There's a demon on the loose. We don't have time to bicker.

I looked directly at Aunt Shannon. "Why is the Reaper in here?"

"To answer the questions that many of us have had since the recent attacks," she said. "Do come in, Head Witch—and you, too, Lady Wildwood."

My mother's expression could have iced over hell itself as she sat down in her usual seat. I sank into mine, wishing I could use my sceptre to freeze the entire council into statues until we caught the demon. Or just Aunt Shannon. I never should have let Maura out of my sight.

"Now we're all here," my aunt said, "the Head Witch will tell us why she failed to inform the rest of the council that a demon was present in Wildwood Heath, and why she brought a Reaper here instead."

Gasps ricocheted up and down the table at the word

demon and then again at *Reaper*. Aunt Shannon wasn't pulling any punches today.

"Maura is assisting the police." I clenched my hands under the table, trying to ignore my mother's warning. "She came here of her own accord, and since two people were killed over the weekend and the attacker was identified as a beast from the afterworld, the police decided to keep her as a consultant. I wasn't involved in their decision."

"Did they now?" said Aunt Shannon. "I didn't know the police hired outsiders to help them."

"It's not unheard of," I said. "Unlike bringing a Reaper into a council meeting. I thought you were adamant that you didn't want any outsiders involving themselves in coven business."

"The attacks *are* coven business," Aunt Shannon said. "I was quite distressed to learn that the evidence of the summoning was found close to my own home and that I was not informed. My children could have been in danger."

Seriously? I bit back a sarcastic response. She'd all but kicked Rowan out of her home herself, and Vanessa was hardly a little kid. She was playing for sympathy, and while the coven members didn't look to have fallen for the act, they also hadn't caused an outcry at the hypocrisy in her dragging Maura into the room. They were all more worried about the demon, and with good reason.

"The police needed time to consider the evidence," I said. "It was closer to my—to Lady Wildwood's property than yours. We didn't want to provoke a panic by announcing the demon's presence to the coven before we knew all the details."

I wished Mum and I had had time to talk through our story beforehand, but I'd little expected my aunt to bring Maura herself here.

"*Is* the demon in the forest?" Aunt Shannon asked. "If so,

then I have to wonder why you aren't more concerned for our safety."

Whispers echoed up and down the table. A middle-aged witch with a pink band in her hair who always spent meetings knitting instead of paying attention spoke up first.

"I didn't hear the Head Witch say the demon was currently in the forest."

"It isn't, and we didn't know it *was* a demon until less than a day ago," I said. "The first two victims were badger shifters who happened to be camping in the woods at the time—"

"The *first* two victims?" Aunt Shannon interjected, her mouth an *o* of feigned shock. "There was another death? You must tell us about it at once."

Again, I had to resist the urge to deploy my sceptre on her. In fact, I would be happy to just thwack her over the head with it without needing to use a spell at all.

"There wasn't another death. A police officer was attacked by someone who he claimed had been possessed at the time, but since it happened less than an hour ago, I didn't have time to verify the facts before I came back here."

Aunt Shannon barely blinked. "I certainly *hope* that our coven isn't the intended target. This seems rather similar to the other incident a few weeks ago, when two Head Witches were tragically attacked in the Wildwood, doesn't it? We do have a lot of enemies."

I would have thought she'd be more reluctant to air our secrets in front of an outsider, but my aunt had been looking for ways to show me up ever since I'd exposed her secret business selling illegal potions online. It wasn't out of the realm of possibility that she'd taken up summoning demons herself and then called a meeting to avoid being blamed, and if I didn't already suspect Tiffany, I would have wholeheartedly jumped on that assumption. Still, Aunt Shannon didn't need to be the instigator to take advantage of the demon's presence in town for her own purposes.

"I quite agree." I mimicked my aunt's affected tone. "That's why police would prefer that as few civilians are aware of this as possible. It would spark a panic, as you can likely imagine, to know that any one of them might be possessed by a dangerous creature at this very moment."

"Possessed?" squeaked one of the other witches. "Is that where the demon is? In town, among us?"

"As far as the police are aware, yes," I said. "Hence why we avoided sharing the details with the public. Provoking the demon into revealing itself will make it more likely to retaliate, and more lives would be needlessly lost."

"Forgive me, Head Witch, but isn't that why you brought the Reaper here?" asked the witch with the pile of knitting on her lap. "To answer our questions?"

Had my aunt given the impression this had been *my* idea?

"I believe Shannon Wildwood is the one who invited the Reaper to attend the meeting, but feel free to ask any questions you have for either of us. It's important that everyone is heard, don't you agree?"

I directed the last part at Aunt Shannon, who gave an insincere smile at my words.

"Naturally, Head Witch. I'm glad to hear you're taking this threat seriously." Aunt Shannon turned to Maura. "Whereabouts do you believe the demon is hiding? Can you find it?"

Maura eyed her. "I believe the demon is possessing someone, and we have a short window before it claims another victim. That would alert me to its location, but I'd prefer to find it before then, wouldn't you?"

Whispers darted up and down the table, but nobody seemed to have taken the hint that she had better things to do than to answer a bunch of questions from the council.

"Claims another victim?" Aunt Shannon echoed. "How concerning. I'm surprised you aren't taking more precautions, Head Witch, if the demon can make the person whom it possesses act against their will."

"Speak for yourself." I caught my mother glaring at me, but she was lucky I hadn't given a less polite reply. "A demon would think twice about drawing attention by possessing the Head Witch. Their goal is mostly to evade detection, which is why we haven't found it yet."

"That's true," Maura said. "Demons want to blend in, first and foremost. They'll only attack someone in public if they're cornered, usually. I hoped to find out if the officer who was attacked earlier was targeted for a particular reason."

"Interesting," Aunt Shannon said. "And you—Reaper—Maura, is it? You came here to hunt the demon?"

"No, I came here because I sensed a summoning spell when I was in the region," she said. "I don't typically get involved in freelance cases, but I figured you didn't have a local Reaper at hand to help, so here I am."

"We don't." Mum finally spoke up. "Which is why I believe that the police could make better use of your help than we can. Don't you agree, Shannon?"

"I was under the impression the police had hit a stalemate," Aunt Shannon said blandly. "I also heard some interesting rumours concerning the Reaper's arrival in town. Is it true that she spent some time in a holding cell?"

She just wouldn't quit.

"Due to the timing of her arrival, the police wanted to question her as a precaution," I said.

"Is that so?" Aunt Shannon replied. "I would have thought the Head Witch could have overruled that choice, since it is an emergency."

Did she *want* me to turn her into a statue?

"We didn't know that at the time. We only became aware that it was a demon attack after the second victim was found. If you want the police's full report, you can call them yourself, but you might have to wait until they have time to spare to answer your questions."

Aunt Shannon's mouth twisted into a smirk. "I was simply interested in how the Head Witch chose to handle the developing situation. I trust you have a plan to ensure the safety of the coven?"

More like she couldn't resist watching me squirm.

"Yes, I do. If you want any sage to put around your office or house, there's an ample supply in the storeroom. The demon is not believed to be possessing anyone in the coven, but if you think someone is acting strangely, tell me at once. Does that cover everything?"

Silence followed. The other witches didn't look entirely satisfied, and I knew I hadn't done the best job trying to sway them back to my side, but Aunt Shannon had made a calculated move to cause maximum disruption, and I had no patience for it.

"If there are no other questions," Mum said, in a tone sharp enough to cut glass, "we'll proceed to the next—"

The door flew open, and Tansy came zipping into the room as if she was being pursued by a giant eagle. When she leapt onto the table and skidded to a halt in front of me, several people jumped to their feet in alarm. Even Aunt Shannon raised her brows at the interruption, while my mother wore an expression that suggested I'd be getting a lecture in decorum the instant the meeting ended.

I ignored her and let my familiar climb onto my arm— Tansy wouldn't have crashed the council meeting unless the situation was urgent. "What is it?"

"There's been another attack!" she squeaked. "In the forest!"

I rose to my feet—no doubt to the confusion of anyone who couldn't understand her squeaking—and asked, "Who?"

"It—your dad—"

Dad. I ran for the door, ignoring the other witches' mutters and gasps.

"Head Witch, what are you doing?" Aunt Shannon called to me, wearing an expression that suggested all her wildest dreams had come true at once.

"I'm going to find the demon, as you so generously suggested." I paused to address the table at large. "I'd appreciate it if the Reaper came with me. The rest of you can consider the meeting to be over."

My aunt's smug expression vanished, and Maura was already on her feet. She and I left the room, and this time Mum didn't call me back. Good. If the demon had hurt my dad—or Jessica and the kids—then decorum could take a swift dive off a cliff.

On the way through the lobby, I ran straight through Grandma's ghost. "Hey!"

"Watch where you're going!" Grandma reached out and *grabbed* me by the arm, almost causing me to lose my balance.

How did she do that?

I wrenched my arm away. "Grandma, this is not the time."

"This is your grandmother?" Maura asked. "She's…"

"Yes, she's a ghost. I know." I skirted around her and walked past my office towards the front door.

Grandma drifted behind me. "You said you wouldn't bring the Reaper here!"

"Blame Aunt Shannon, not me."

Just like all my other problems. If my aunt hadn't hijacked the meeting and forced Maura and me to sit through her questioning, we might have been able to catch the demon before it targeted my other family members.

"I have no intention of banishing you, only the demon," Maura told Grandma. "I don't suppose you've seen it?"

"The cheek of it." Grandma looked affronted. "I have no intention of ever going near a demon again."

"What do you mean, *again*?" Maura asked, but I didn't stop to hear the answer.

Once outside the coven's headquarters, I began a sprint towards the forest entrance.

"Your brother's already here," Tansy squeaked in my ear. "He said Jessica called him."

"He did?" I gasped out the words, worst-case scenarios running rampant through my mind. "What exactly happened to Dad?"

"He—I don't know, but I think he was possessed. That's what your brother said."

Dad. Fear and anger clenched my heart. He hadn't deserved to be dragged into this at all, let alone used as a plaything by a demon.

"What is your familiar saying?" Maura asked from behind me. "I don't speak squirrel."

"My dad was possessed." Voicing the words aloud made fresh urgency spur me onward, despite my aching legs and screaming lungs. "His partner has two small children. They live near where the first body was discovered, but I don't know—I don't know how the demon found them."

Tansy leapt off my shoulder and disappeared among the trees in a bright-red blur, while I wished I had Maura's ability to hop through the shadows to catch up to her.

Maura herself continued to walk alongside me. "I don't want to scare the demon and make it worse," she explained. "Since I don't know exactly where it is anyway, I'll have to sneak up on it."

I nodded, too breathless to speak, and continued towards my dad's cottage. When we reached the small house, the first thing I noticed was my brother. He stood outside alone, and two pale and terrified faces peered from the window. Jessica stood in front of the doorway, and Dad...

He lay on the ground at Ramsey's feet. Not moving.

"Ramsey," I gasped. "What the hell is this?"

"He was possessed," Ramsey said quietly. "I had to stop him, and... I don't know if my banishment spell worked."

"I'd take a guess that it didn't," Maura said from behind me, but Ramsey didn't seem to even notice her.

I halted to catch my breath. "You knocked him out?"

"I didn't know what else to do."

I'd never heard my brother sound so uncertain in my life.

"I didn't dare wake him up in case the demon was still there," he said.

"Maura can help." I swallowed, my throat dry. "Did you bring any sage with you?"

"Yes." Ramsey reached into his pocket with a mechanically jerky motion.

Had he not even brought any other officers with him? Why hadn't he thought of getting the sage out sooner? Shock must have slowed his usually sharp mind, and when his fingers fumbled and dropped the plastic bag of sage, I scooped it up.

Questions later. Help Dad first. My own hands trembled as I sprinkled sage in a circle around my dad's unconscious body, while Jessica watched with haunted eyes.

"Can you help him?" she whispered. "Will he be okay?"

"Yeah." God, I hoped so. "Maura knows what she's doing. Are the kids okay?"

"I shut them in the house when I realised he was possessed." She squeezed her eyes shut, her hands clenching. "I... couldn't take the risk."

"That was quick thinking." With the sage circle complete,

I stepped back. "It'll be fine. He'll be back home before you know it." My voice wavered less than I'd expected.

Jessica swallowed and nodded. Good. I wanted her and the kids to be okay even if the unthinkable happened. Wrenching my gaze away, I looked to Maura, who surveyed Dad's unconscious form with her brow furrowed.

"What are you doing?" I gestured at the sage I'd sprinkled on the forest floor. "Are you going to use a banishment spell, or should I?"

My brother stepped in. "I can handle it."

"A banishment won't work if the demon is still possessing him," Maura said. "We need to scare it into letting go of him first."

"How?" I watched in confusion as Maura paced around the sage circle, stopping behind my brother.

Then she shoved Ramsey forward and into the circle of sage.

Ramsey staggered in shock, while I lifted my sceptre.

"What the hell are you doing?" I asked.

"The demon is possessing him. It switched hosts."

"How dare you?" Ramsey caught his balance and spun towards Maura, fury in his gaze.

"Don't try to hide, demon." Maura's voice gained an odd, echoing quality, and the shadows around her feet thickened, rising upward as if they'd gained a life of their own.

In response, Ramsey's eyes went flat black, and the pupils disappeared altogether. Instead of my brother, something else entirely watched from his eyes.

My breath caught. She was right. My brother was possessed by a demon.

13

The monster watched from my brother's eyes, and the pitch-darkness bleeding outward from his pupils brought a shudder to my very bones.

"Get away from him." I found my voice. "Get away from my brother."

My brother remained still, his expression eerily calm as he stood beside my dad, both of them encircled by the sage I'd sprinkled on the ground. *The sage is keeping the demon contained.* But that didn't mean it would let go of Ramsey without a fight.

"Maura," I hissed between my teeth, lifting the sceptre. "Do something. Before—"

As the sceptre's purple glow travelled over my brother's face, he recoiled and a dark blur detached itself from his body like a large bird taking flight, reforming itself into a human-sized figure made of shadows.

I watched in horror as the dark figure lunged at me—and then halted as if it had collided with invisible glass. Ramsey slumped to his knees inside the circle of the sage, while the shadowy mass recoiled when Maura approached it.

"You're scared of both of us, aren't you?" she said conversationally. "Give it up, demon. Go back into the afterworld."

A glow ignited in her eyes, and when she reached towards the circle, shadows encased her fingertips. The demon shuffled further back, but thanks to the sage, it had nowhere to run to.

"Go!" Maura pointed at the demon with shadowy fingers, her voice ringing in the air like a bell.

At her command, the dark patch shrank from human-sized to scarcely bigger than the palm of my hand before winking out of existence altogether. I didn't need to be able to see the afterworld to know the demon was gone, and utter stillness remained in its place. The forest was quiet, cold, and I became aware of the goose bumps on my arms and the sceptre trembling in my hands. Dad lay unconscious, oblivious to Ramsey kneeling at his side, unspeaking.

"Ramsey." I dropped to a crouch. "Talk to me."

He lifted his head, and relief washed over me when I saw his own eyes looking back at me instead of those inhuman black pits. His gaze then filled with horror when he saw Dad's unconscious body.

"Robin." He licked his lips. "What—?"

"You were possessed," said Maura, without any sympathy. "You probably have gaps in your memory, but if I had to guess, your father was possessed first. The demon then hopped into your body when you knocked him out."

"I... remember." He climbed to his feet, unsteadily. "But it's hazy."

"That would be the demon." Maura nodded to the sage at his feet. "You're safe to step out of the circle now. The demon's gone."

Ramsey stumbled a few steps then turned to Dad. "I'll wake him up."

"Wait." Maura held out a hand. "Make sure he's inside the sage circle first."

"Why?" I moved to obey her command all the same, nudging Dad's arm into the sage circle. "The demon is gone…"

"There might be another," added Maura. "Not likely, but it's better that we take precautions."

"You think there were two?" I helped Ramsey move Dad the rest of the way into the circle. I'd never seen him so quick to follow someone else's instructions, and it said volumes for how the situation must have shaken him up.

"It's unlikely, but you never know." Maura nodded to Ramsey. "Wake him up."

Ramsey flicked his wand. Dad stirred, and a second wave of relief hit me so hard that my knees trembled. Jessica moved forward, her hand over her mouth, as Dad slowly lifted his head and looked around in confusion.

"What…? How'd I get here?"

I looked to Ramsey, but he said nothing, as if his mouth was stapled shut. I swallowed hard. "Dad… don't you remember anything?"

"No… I went out to do a job for someone this morning, but I don't remember coming back." His gaze went to the house, where Jake and Spike's faces were pressed against the living room window. "What's going on?"

"You were possessed," I told him. "By a demon."

Dawning horror rippled over his face. "I didn't hurt Jessica or the kids, did I?"

Ramsey gave a violent headshake. "No—no, you didn't. Jessica called the police because you were acting strangely, and I came here at once."

"Matthew!" Jessica gasped Dad's name and threw her arms around him. "You're all right. I was so worried."

Ramsey's mouth slammed shut. Part of me wanted to encourage him to keep talking, to seize on the chance to bond with them both in the moment of solidarity, but I could scarcely get a grip on my own emotions. I turned to Maura instead, who'd retreated to give them some space, while Tansy emerged from where she'd been hiding under a bush and scrambled up my arm.

"Is that it?" Tansy whispered in my ear. "Is the demon gone?"

"Apparently so," I whispered back. "Unless—Maura, *do* you think there were two?"

"Only if the summoner has a death wish," Maura said. "No, you should figure out how it got at your dad first. I'm guessing the demon must have hopped from that camper into another host and then caught your dad on his way home, but I don't know for sure."

"Sounds right." I might have been able to come up with another theory myself, but the close call had shaken me up almost as much as Ramsey, and I couldn't think clearly at all. "Hey—Ramsey, where are you going?"

He'd begun to walk away from Dad's house, head bowed. "I never did set those campers free, and since I ran off alone, I need to explain everything to my officers. This is on me."

I moved to catch up to him. "Ramsey, I'm pretty sure this is the sort of situation where it's understandable that you'd run off alone. Your officers will understand."

"I was *possessed*, Robin." He spoke through gritted teeth. "I might have hurt or killed someone."

"It's more likely that you'd have been killed by the demon yourself," Maura told him.

"Not helping." Despite my gratitude for the way she'd saved his neck, I wished she'd have a bit more tact. "Where's *your* brother?"

"Hiding," she replied. "He doesn't like demons."

"Neither do I," Tansy announced from my shoulder. "I find it hard to believe that monster was ever human."

"You said demons were like ghosts," I added to Maura. "That *thing* did not remotely resemble a ghost."

"They're both spirits," she said. "I did say demons are a long way from the humans they used to be."

"That's one way of putting it." At the sound of retreating footsteps, I faced my brother. "Ramsey—"

"I have to go." He kept walking, without looking back. "Sorry."

I called his name, but he ignored me. Outside the cottage, Dad and Jessica stood conversing in low voices. Perhaps they were trying to figure out how to explain the events to the kids.

"I guess we should go," Maura said. "Do I have to come back to the coven meeting?"

"No, but I do." I'd completely forgotten the mess I'd left behind at the coven's headquarters. "How'd you end up there in the first place? Did Aunt Shannon ambush you in the middle of town?"

"Pretty much," she replied. "She made it sound as if I had an exclusive invitation to a meeting."

"Or an excuse to make me look like a fool in front of the council," I muttered. "My mother warned me she was scheming. I should have listened, but one would think the demon would take precedence."

"I've met her sort before," she said. "Your aunt, I mean. Not that I know your family well, but do you think *she* might have summoned the demon?"

"She's awful," I said, "but summoning demons isn't her style."

"I guess that's your brother's job," she said. "To find the summoner."

"Yeah." Whoever it was, the fact that my dad had been the

demon's target felt decidedly personal. The demon itself hadn't said a word to give away who'd summoned it, though. "As for me, I need to go back to work."

As little as I wanted to go near the office, Aunt Shannon would have less reason to undermine me again if I told the council we'd got rid of the demon and the threat was over. My mother would be less than satisfied, but if we wanted to unmask the summoner, I needed the coven on my side.

As Maura left, I caught Dad's eye. He gave me a strained smile, while Jessica unlocked the cottage door.

"You have to go back to work, don't you?" Dad asked.

"Yeah… You'll be okay?" I blinked, my eyes stinging, as the two kids threw themselves out of the door and dragged him and Jessica into a group hug.

"Of course," he said. "Drop by later if you have time."

"Yeah—I will."

Mum would likely want me to stay at the office to give a blow-by-blow account of the fight with the demon to the council, but I refused point-blank to stay after hours to answer a million questions from Aunt Shannon. Family came before decorum, always.

"How'd you find out what was going on?" I asked Tansy as we left the cottage behind.

"I got bored of chasing that magpie around the garden, so I went into the forest," she said. "I saw your brother running towards your dad's house and followed him, but when I saw your dad—he wasn't himself."

She didn't need to say more. The demon hadn't been anything like I'd expected, and the fear that it had evoked from the knowledge that it had control over my family members was unlike anything I'd experienced before. "I hope we've seen the last of it."

"Me too."

Sensing I needed moral support, Tansy remained sitting on my shoulder as I walked into the headquarters, instead of running to the back garden as she normally did.

I'd expected my mother to ambush me at the door, but she was nowhere to be seen, and the open door to the council meeting room revealed it was empty. Frowning, I opened the door to my office. An abrupt silence hit me as several voices stopped talking at the same instant. Mum, Grandma's ghost, and Chloe all turned my way when I walked into the room, but only Chloe greeted me.

"Ah—Robin. You're back."

"The demon has gone." I directed my words at Mum. "It possessed my dad and then Ramsey, but Maura managed to get rid of it without anyone being hurt."

Mum stared at me. "Ramsey? Are you sure?"

"Yes, I'm sure." If I hadn't witnessed the scene with my own eyes, I might have taken it for an elaborate nightmare, but the cold rawness scraping at my insides lingered longer than the aftereffects of a dream. "It possessed Dad first, and when Jessica realised and called the police, Ramsey went straight there from the office. He knocked Dad out with a spell, but that's all Tansy saw before she came to warn me."

"The Reaper banished the demon, did she?"

Mum's tone was calm, but Chloe goggled from the sidelines, and even Grandma looked uncharacteristically grim.

"With her powers?" Mum asked.

"Yes."

The demon had been scared of the sceptre, too, but if not for Maura, I didn't know that I could have banished it myself. "If we hadn't left the meeting when we did, one or both of them would be dead. If you want me to tell your sister that, I will."

Mum's mouth pressed into a thin line. "I don't agree with

what my sister did, but you should have expected her to object to you working with the Reaper without telling the council."

"My brother had Maura locked up as a suspect until yesterday," I pointed out. "How exactly would I have explained *that* to the council?"

"Regardless, you acted alone, and you were taken to account for it."

"I can't believe you're taking her side." My fear dimmed as a wave of furious indignation arose to take its place. "The demon nearly killed Ramsey—your own *son*—and if we hadn't got there when we did, it might have succeeded. Would you rather we'd stayed for a Q&A with Aunt Shannon instead?"

"Calm down, Robin," Mum said. "That wasn't what I meant. I was commenting on your insistence on acting as you see fit when you're the head of a team to whom you owe accountability."

"Did you want me to bring the entire coven to face the demon?" I tried and failed to reel in my temper. "I don't remember Grandma lining up her coven members for her enemies to use as target practise."

"Keep *me* out of your arguments," Grandma said. "If the demon is gone, we can return to the usual procedure."

"The hell we can," I said heatedly. "The summoner is still out there, remember? Since the last time Ramsey took the situation into his own hands, he got himself possessed, I'd prefer not to leave this up to the police alone. If not for Maura, there's no telling what the demon might have done to him."

I didn't want to contemplate it, truth be told, but I didn't know how else to convince Mum and Grandma that there were more important matters at stake than whether I followed the rulebook. As for the rest of the council, I hardly cared what they thought.

Mum's eyes narrowed. "I don't need you to manipulate me with guilt, Robin."

"Aunt Shannon is the manipulator, which you know perfectly well," I said. "She set me up."

"Too easily."

"What was I supposed to do, go straight to the office and call a meeting when Jessica found the body?" I asked. "We didn't know a demon had killed that shifter at first. You thought it was a false alarm, remember?"

"I never believed that, Robin," she said. "I did believe someone intended to cause the coven to panic without knowing the full picture."

"Yeah, and on that note, what if it's not coincidental that the body turned up near my dad's house?" I asked. "Targeting him is an obvious way to get at me without running up against the coven. It's the sort of thing the Henbanes would do, and I don't see you rushing to blame *them* for any of this."

"There are thirty-five registered members of their coven," Mum said. "Questioning all of them will take time, and that's certainly the police's job."

"Yes, and if you want to lecture anyone about acting alone, Ramsey's right there." I made my way to my desk chair and sank into it. "Otherwise, I'll stay here. Is that all? What else do you want me to do?"

"Nothing," Mum said. "Other than for you to return to your work for the duration of the day."

As she left the room, Tansy wrapped her tail around my neck like a fluffy scarf, while Chloe cleared her throat.

"I'm sorry about your brother, Robin. And your dad," Chloe said.

"They're okay." I rested my head in my hands. "Well, they're alive."

I might have asked what she and Mum had been discussing with Grandma, but I didn't have the mental space to deal with the notion of them talking about me behind my back. I hoped Mum had an equally intense lecture saved up for Ramsey, but that might be hoping for too much.

My phone began to buzz. With a groan, I lifted my head from my hands and checked the number. Harvey. Ah, screw it. If my mother came to reprimand me for taking a call from my boyfriend during the workday, so be it.

"Hey." I answered the phone. "Did you hear?"

"I just saw the police heading into the forest," he said. "When they shut down the playing field yesterday, I was worried. What happened?"

"My dad got possessed. Then my brother." My head throbbed. "The demon—Maura banished it, don't worry. It's gone."

"They what?" Horror filled his voice. "Are they okay?"

"They're fine, but I had to go straight back to work." I rubbed my temples with my free hand. "I'll explain in more detail later. I'm kind of in the doghouse with my mother for skipping out on a council meeting to chase down the demon."

"That's ridiculous," he said. "The demon's gone, though?"

"According to Maura, yes," I said. "We need to find the summoner, though, before they get back on their feet and try again."

"That's up to your brother, right?"

"Once he's recovered from the shock."

"Oh. I guess he didn't take it well?"

"Yeah, he took off the instant Dad recovered, presumably to bury himself in work for the rest of the day. I'm not allowed to leave my office yet, but I'll go there after work."

I'd intended to check on Dad, too, but at least he had

Jessica and the kids to keep him company. Ramsey, though…
he'd need a wake-up call to get him out of the office, and I
was more than happy to deliver.

"Are you sure *you're* okay?" asked Harvey.

"Of course."

Was I? Nobody else had been willing to comfort me
except Tansy. But now I was on the phone with the one
person who hadn't been involved *and* who held no judge-
ment against me, and I'd found myself trying to reassure him
instead of the other way around. That was what the Head
Witch was supposed to do, I knew, but maybe I'd absorbed
the expectations a little too well.

"I'll be fine," I added. "I just need to get through this
paperwork. After the demon, it'll be a bit of light relief."

"If you're sure," he said. "See you later?"

"Absolutely." I ended the call and went back to the pile of
documents.

Tansy tried to cheer me up by bouncing around the office
and annoying Carmilla, Grandma's cat. My grandmother
herself had vanished when Mum had left and neither showed
up again that afternoon, which was probably for the best. I'd
have to apologise for losing my temper with her, but it would
have been nice if she was a little more understanding.

Once I was finally free from the office, I headed to the
police station with Tansy sitting on my shoulder as a
comforting presence. The warm streets of Wildwood Heath
were a balm to my tense mood, and Tansy ran to chase a
flock of pigeons as I approached the police station's doors.

"If you're looking for your brother, he just went out," said
Julian. From the smell lingering around his desk, he'd
covered half the office in sage.

"He did?" *Please tell me he went to question the Henbanes.*
"Alone?"

"I believe he went to see Seth at the hospital."

"Right." I'd forgotten his fellow officer had been ambushed earlier. "I'll go and find him."

"You won't be allowed in," Julian called after me as the doors slid closed behind my back.

I'd hardly taken two steps before Maura appeared out of the shadows in front of me.

"Whoa." I held a hand to my racing heart. "I thought you didn't do that in public."

Maura's gaze roved around the street. "I sensed a demon summoning."

"Another one?" My mouth went dry. "Where? My brother's at the hospital…"

"Why?"

"He's visiting Seth, who was attacked by the last person who got possessed…" I paced away from the police station. "Not Dad, but the person before him."

I think. My heart began pounding in my ears, and adrenaline surged in my blood as I took off at a run. Tansy leapt onto my shoulder and clung to me as we ran for the hospital. Luckily it wasn't far, and when we entered, I found several staff members in the reception area.

"Hey—where's my brother?" I asked the nearest person.

"Head Witch." The nurse, an Asian woman with cropped hair, eyed my sceptre with typical awe. "Your brother just left to find Seth. We planned to keep him for observation because of that nasty-looking bite of his, but he ran off without being discharged."

"Where?" I backed into the doorway, heart lurching. "Was Seth acting weirdly? Different than usual?"

The nurse gave me an odd look. "Well, he ran out of here without saying a word to anyone. Does that count?"

My skin chilled. I turned to Maura, whose expression was grim. "Do you think…?"

"Yeah." She backed out of the hospital and began to walk away. "I'd say the odds are high that he was possessed."

Seth was possessed. Had Ramsey figured it out and intended to confront him alone? Hadn't he learned his lesson from earlier?

Mind reeling, I retraced my steps to the police station on autopilot, where Julian blinked at me from behind his desk.

"You missed him again," he said. "Your brother was just here, not a minute ago, but he took off like a bat out of hell."

"He was?" *Why did he come back?* "Was Seth here? He's supposed to be at the hospital…"

"I know," said Julian. "He was here right before you, but he didn't stick around. I think Ramsey was looking for him."

I saw a couple of officers inside the waiting room and went to intercept them. "Hey—did either of you see Seth when he came in? A few minutes ago?"

Shana, one of the officers, glowered at me. "You might be Head Witch, but that doesn't entitle you to walk in and out of here whenever you feel like. If you want your brother, he already left."

"Did he tell you he was possessed earlier?"

"Did he *what?*"

Dammit, Ramsey. "He was, and I think Seth is too. He was here, right?"

The colour drained from her face. "Yes, and he went to the secure room where we keep anything confiscated from our prisoners."

My heart plunged in my chest. "Like the Henbanes."

Hadn't my brother been studying the books they'd confiscated? That might be the least of what the police had found in their house, but it didn't explain why Maura had sensed a summoning spell when the demon had already been possessing Seth.

Ignoring Julian and Shana's questions, I ran for the door,

grabbing Maura's arm as I did so. Her skin was ice-cold, but I hardly noticed.

My brother was about to take on the demon alone, and this time he might not be lucky enough to escape alive.

14

I took off at a run, while Maura jogged beside me. "Where are you going?"

"To find my brother." I kept up the pace, dodging passers-by who were either leaving their offices or running errands on the way back from work. "Can you track where that summoning spell came from?"

"It took me by surprise, so no," she replied. "I can take us to your brother. That might be easier."

"Take us?"

I halted when shadows swept from her hands like smoke, swirling around both of us. Tansy gripped my shoulder, her fur standing on end.

"Wait—you can take other people through the shadows too?"

"I'm not strictly supposed to take passengers along for the ride," said Maura, "but it's not like anyone's keeping tabs on me."

"Where'd your brother go?" I asked.

"Mart's hiding in his room at the inn," she said. "I told you he doesn't like demons."

"I'm surprised anyone does."

The shadows surging around Maura's palms looked entirely too similar to the dark creature she'd banished earlier, but if she could get me to my brother's side in an instant, I'd have to face the fear.

"How does it work? You step through the shadows and appear in a specific location?"

"I can also take us to a specific person," she said. "Provided I've met them already, which I have. I guess I'll have to thank your brother for arresting me."

"Wow." I drew in a breath as she moved closer to me, a chill brushing my neck. "Tell me what to do."

"You have to hold on to me," she replied. "Or else you'll get lost in the afterworld. I'd also advise you not to bring your familiar."

Tansy shivered against my neck. "I don't want *you* to go either, Robin."

"I'll be fine," I told her, though I wasn't sure, at all. "You go and tell Mum that Ramsey has decided to go off and be a hero again—then warn Dad there's another demon."

"All right." She nuzzled my chin and then hopped off my shoulder, landing on all fours outside the shadows pooling at Maura's feet.

In the meantime, I gripped the sceptre in one hand and extended the other towards Maura. "I have to hold your hand?"

"Nah, just grab my shoulder or something," she said. "Don't let go, though. I wasn't kidding when I said you might end up lost in the afterworld if you do."

Hesitantly, I grabbed her upper arm, shivering at the coldness emanating from her whole body. Then shadows rose from Maura's hands and swallowed both of us.

Utter darkness masked our surroundings. If not for the purplish glow of the sceptre in my hand, I wouldn't be able to see anything at all. Even Maura had almost become part of the shadows herself, despite the solid feeling of her arm in my grip. The cold stole the breath from my lungs, while the darkness seemed to have no end. No wonder Grandma wanted to spend all her time in the waking world instead of the afterworld.

I concentrated on the purple glow of my sceptre penetrating the darkness to avoid losing my nerve, and after several endless seconds, the darkness receded. Thick forest surrounded us, and I pried my fingers loose from Maura's arm.

"Robin?" Ramsey stood in front of us, baffled. "Where did you come from?"

"We took a short cut." I rubbed my chilled arms. "Seth is possessed, right? Where is he?"

"How did you—right, the Reaper." He ran a hand through his hair, his gaze flicking towards Maura. "He's somewhere in the forest, but he moved so fast I couldn't keep up with him. I should have known there was something wrong with him, but I assumed there was one demon, not two."

"So did I." I lifted my cold hand and punched him in the arm. "Why in the goddess's name did you decide to go chasing after him alone? Again? For crying out loud, Ramsey, you should know better."

"He stole the books, Robin." He rubbed his arm but didn't reprimand me for hitting him, a sure sign that the apocalypse was nigh. "I didn't have time to explain everything to the rest of my officers. Most of them can't see demons."

"That doesn't mean you have to take it down single-handedly." I turned to Maura. "Can you sense it?"

"The demon?" she asked. "No, but there might be more than one if that summoning spell I sensed was used to summon another demon, which is likely."

"What?" The colour drained from Ramsey's face.

"Another summoning spell? Robin—is the Reaper telling the truth?"

"Maura," I said. "Her name is Maura, and yes, she can help us get rid of both demons if you just calm down."

"Calm down?" He paced ahead, tugging his hand through his hair. "Seth is possessed, and if someone else used a summoning spell—"

"That doesn't mean you have to act alone." I faced Maura. "What do you think? If the demon's too far away to sense, we can go to the Henbanes' headquarters and hope we find it there."

"If you're sure one of them summoned it," Maura said. "I can track Seth, but if he's possessed and we land on top of him, that's a recipe for disaster."

"Do it." Ramsey had a slightly manic glint in his eyes, and given the strong smell of sage in the air, he must have grabbed some from the police station.

I raised a brow at him. "You want to take a short cut through the shadows?"

"There's no need." Maura stiffened, her gaze fixed ahead, as if she was looking at something none of the rest of us could see. "He's close."

"Alive?" Ramsey wheeled around as Maura took off at a fast stride, and we hurried to catch up to her.

Now that I recognised our surroundings, I realised we hadn't gone far into the Wildwood at all. My mother's house was barely a two-minute walk away.

"We're near the Henbanes' place," I said to Ramsey. "Hey—"

I skidded to a halt when we rounded a corner and found Maura had stopped in her tracks. In front of us, Seth stood in the middle of the path, his wand in his hand and an expression of bewilderment on his face.

"Head Witch." His gaze roved from me to my brother. "What are you all doing in here?"

"I could ask you the same question," I said. "Do you remember being possessed by a demon?"

"You might still be possessed," added Maura. "Anyone got some sage?"

"Hang on," Seth said.

Seth backed up a step as Ramsey reached into his pocket.

"I don't know what's going on, but the last thing I remember is being in my hospital bed. How'd I get here?"

"A demon was possessing you," I explained. "Probably since you brought those two campers to the police station."

If that was when the demon had jumped hosts, it would explain Ralph's memory issues and why it hadn't killed him. There'd been witnesses, and I'd bet it had seen a police officer as a more useful host.

Maura narrowed her eyes at Seth. "Demon, show yourself."

"He's not possessed," I said.

His confusion seemed genuine enough, though I didn't know why the demon had spared him.

"Seth, did you run into anyone else in the woods?"

"No, I told you I don't remember anything since being in the hospital." His voice trembled. "How can I have been possessed? I'm still alive."

"Got lucky, I guess," said Maura. "The demon must have had you bring the book to its summoner, but I don't know why it let you go."

"Can you sense it anywhere nearby?" I asked.

Maura shook her head. "It must have claimed another host already. That makes it harder to track."

"What if a non-Reaper goes after it?" Ramsey asked. "Can we draw it into a trap?"

"Ramsey, you need to drop the idea of fighting alone," I

told him. "Especially if there's more than one. Let's see what the Henbanes have been up to."

I headed towards the houses that backed to the forest, but a sudden roar hit my ears. Maura swore, while Seth exclaimed in alarm, his gaze on the treetops.

"What *is* that?"

Good question. Darkness bled into the sky ahead of us, and through a gap in the trees, I glimpsed a large shaggy shape that resembled the one that still haunted my nightmares, weeks after I'd last seen it.

A Ghast.

Ramsey pulled out his wand, while I raised the sceptre. Maura cursed again as two identical beasts emerged from the shadows and charged into the forest.

I backed up a step, raising the sceptre, and one of the semi-transparent beasts came crashing through the woodland. A spell lit up the air—courtesy of Ramsey—and the beast momentarily froze, but a chorus of snarls came from the bushes. One of the other beasts swatted at Maura, who hopped into the shadows and then reappeared directly behind the Ghast. As she lunged, the beast recoiled, its heavy body shaking the trees around us.

I looked for the third beast and saw it running in the opposite direction… towards my family's house. I made to follow, but a guttural snarl indicated the beast Ramsey had hit with a spell had shaken off its temporary paralysis. With a wave of my sceptre, I immobilised the beast, begrudgingly glad of Grandma's often brutal lessons.

As the Ghast froze, Maura shouted, "Get out!"

Her voice vibrated with power, and the shadows rose, swallowing her opponent whole. Darkness flowed from her hands, swathing the beast, and when it vanished, no traces of the Ghast remained.

The one I'd paralysed remained statue-like, but the other

continued to rampage towards the houses, leaving a trail of broken branches in its wake.

"Maura, where are you going?" I took aim at the beast's back with my sceptre but missed, while Maura ran straight past it.

"To stop whoever summoned those monsters!" Maura said over her shoulder. "I guess it's better than a second demon, but that doesn't mean they won't try that next."

"And the first one?"

It might have left Seth alone, but what if it had gone after Dad again? Or Mum? I hoped Tansy had managed to warn at least one of them, but even Maura's shadow-hopping ability couldn't help me be in two places at once.

Instead of answering, Maura vanished into the shadows. Ramsey, meanwhile, was already charging after the rampaging Ghast, while Seth jogged behind me, no doubt more to get out of the line of fire than out of any desire to fight the monsters. I didn't blame him.

As we circled the backs of the houses, a loud shout reached my ears. Hang on—was that Aunt Shannon? With a burst of speed, I emerged from the forest path and onto the road, where darkness swathed the sky directly above the Henbanes' back garden—and the coven's headquarters.

Mum. Ramsey and I shared one grim look as we ran, straight to the coven headquarters. With the sceptre aglow in my hands and my lungs screaming, I burst into the lobby.

Someone screamed from the back garden, prompting Ramsey and me to run in that direction. Outside, Aunt Shannon stood rooted to the spot as the Ghast stalked towards her.

Upon hearing our approach, she shouted, "Get rid of that beast at once, Head Witch."

"You have a wand, don't you?" Not that there was anyone

else to back her up; the rest of the coven must have already left for home.

I pointed the sceptre at the beast, casting a freezing charm that caused it to halt in the middle of the lawn.

"We need to banish it," I said to Ramsey. "You have sage with you?"

He dug a hand into his pocket. "Yes, but not enough for both monsters—and the demon."

"Maura's probably dealing with it." I held out a hand, wishing I'd had the presence of mind to raid the supply cupboards myself.

Ramsey handed me a plastic bag of sage and approached the beast, which lay sprawled on the lawn. As I joined him, I kept an eye on the darkness swathing the Henbane Coven's garden.

"What is going on over there?" I asked.

"Something nasty, no doubt."

Ramsey stiffened as a roar came from near the forest, and a moment later, I glimpsed the third beast barrelling through the maze at the back of the garden.

"Robin—"

"On it."

I lifted the sceptre as the beast charged, and my freezing spell caused the Ghast to halt next to its companion on the lawn.

"Nicely done," said Ramsey, in a compliment that I doubted would ever be repeated in my life. "We can banish them both at once."

"Yes, and I'd appreciate it if *someone* else would lend a hand." I pointedly addressed Aunt Shannon. "Where's my mother?"

When she didn't answer, I glanced behind me and saw that she'd retreated into the coven's headquarters and closed the door. *And to think she tried to make* me *look bad.*

Ramsey and I finished sprinkling sage in a circle around the two beasts, at which point I lifted my sceptre. "We might need more than two of us to banish them."

"Three." Seth came running out of the building behind us. "More, once the backup I called gets here."

"Thank you," Ramsey said. "That was good thinking."

Seth looked startled at the praise. "No problem. What do you want me to do, Head Witch?"

It was my turn to be startled. "A regular banishment spell will do. We'll try on three. One, two—"

Light shot from my sceptre and the others' wands, colliding above the beasts, but the pair of them didn't vanish. *There aren't enough of us.* As I'd feared.

"Do we need the Reaper's help?" Seth guessed. "Is she… dealing with that? Whatever it is?"

I followed his gaze towards the patch of darkness above the Henbane Coven's garden. "We can do it without her if we have enough volunteers. Who wants to fetch Aunt Shannon?"

"She's here." Ramsey jerked his head towards the house, where our aunt had emerged.

"What are you doing?" Aunt Shannon backed away from someone, her wand held high. "Stop that at once!"

Mum walked out of the building behind her, and my blood chilled when I saw the flat blackness in her eyes. The demon had possessed my mother.

15

"Head Witch," Mum said—or the demon did. The voice sounded like hers, but it was entirely cold and flat, devoid of emotion. "You aren't supposed to be here."

"What's that mean?" I stared straight into the demon's pitch-black eyes. "Aren't I your target? That's why you keep possessing my family members, isn't it?"

I lifted the sceptre, but the demon recoiled before I could begin to cast a spell. Mum staggered forward as the patch of darkness detached itself from her, resolving into its humanoid form. Was it afraid of the sceptre?

The demon had undeniably recognised me, but as I opened my mouth to speak, Maura emerged from the shadows.

"There you are." She ran towards the demon, which vanished in a blur of darkness.

Whoa, that was fast.

"That wasn't you, was it?" I asked Maura. "It ran off."

"It's gone into hiding in the afterworld." She eyed my

mother, who'd sunk to her knees in a way that mirrored Ramsey after he'd been possessed.

The sight of her usually controlled manner broken in such a way was surreal enough that I almost forgot about the Ghasts until Ramsey cleared his throat.

"Reaper—can you banish those?"

"Three of us wasn't enough," I explained. "Maura, can you help?"

"Sure." She paced towards the two beasts, while Ramsey and Seth watched from the sidelines, their wands in their hands.

I lifted my sceptre too. "Why would the demon be afraid of my sceptre? I assume it wasn't *me* that terrified it so much."

"I can't say I know much about sceptres," Maura said. "It's a giant overpowered wand, right?"

"Yes, but shouldn't it have been more afraid of you?"

"Reapers are harder to run from." She reached the circle of sage that encased the two Ghasts. "I wonder if the summoner brought out these monsters *because* the demon is afraid of the sceptre? These brutes don't know any better. They'll attack anyone, even a Reaper."

"Robin!" Mum was back on her feet. "What *is* going on here?"

"We have it under control. Kind of." An inexplicable sense of relief flooded me at the sight of her usual stern expression. "Do you remember being possessed?"

"Do I remember *what*?" Her eyes widened. "The last thing I remember is your familiar coming into my office to warn me there was a second demon, and when I left, I ran into..."

"Me," Seth said. "I remember now."

"The demon changed hosts then," I concluded. "Seth brought the books... but what did you do with them?"

"What books?" Mum's eyes bulged when she saw the

darkness simmering over the Henbane Coven's garden. "And just what is going on over there?"

"They're the ones behind this." I gestured at the circle of sage and the beasts within. "Turns out there was a second demon, and I bet they're working on summoning more."

Shadows engulfed the two beasts trapped within the circle as Maura worked her magic, and Mum watched for a moment too.

"She really does know what she's doing, then," Mum said.

"You don't say?" I frowned at her. "Also, why would the demon be afraid of my sceptre?"

To my bafflement, she averted her gaze. "It's complicated. I'll explain later."

"What are you talking about?"

Before she could answer, Maura vanished in a shadowy blur, and Mum took a step back. "Where'd she go?"

"To find the demon, I hope." I swivelled to the fence dividing our garden from its neighbour and saw Ramsey take a step in that direction. "Don't you even think about going over there alone."

"If that's where Maura is, I won't be alone," he said. "What was that about your sceptre?"

"It scared the demon," I said. "Mum said it's complicated. Is that news to you?"

He remained fixated on the Henbanes' garden. "No doubt demons are intelligent enough to know the sceptre is a beacon that can banish them back to the afterworld."

"Been reading up on demons, have you?" Grandma's ghost appeared, hovering above the lawn, and everyone except Mum jumped.

I pointed the sceptre at her. "How long have you been there?"

"Since my daughter got possessed," she said. "You didn't think I'd let a demon get into my home, did you?"

"I thought you were hiding." My last thread of patience for the former Head Witch evaporated. "You know, it would have been nice if we'd had someone in the afterworld who could have warned us that the Henbanes were conducting necromancy right next to our headquarters."

"That's enough cheek from you," she said. "I couldn't have warned you because I didn't know. I didn't think that demon would be fool enough to come back."

"What do you mean by that?" I rotated towards Mum, who eyed her mother's ghost with a mixture of surprise and resignation. "Was she consorting with demons in her free time as Head Witch?"

"Don't be absurd," said Mum. "Your grandmother... she ought to explain this herself."

"Explain what?"

The question came from Ramsey, and his evident confusion told me that even he didn't know what our mother and grandmother were talking about. That was a first.

"In her time as Head Witch, your grandmother made some powerful enemies," Mum said slowly.

"I know *that*," I said. "Including the Henbanes, which is why I don't understand why you didn't suspect them of meddling with demons."

"Not them," Grandma said impatiently. "I thought you were more intelligent than that."

"It's the demon," Ramsey said. "You've met it before. Haven't you?"

"Which one?"

I swivelled to my grandmother. "Don't they look exactly the same?"

"You didn't ask their names?"

"Demons have names?" Maura had said that every demon had been human once, but she'd also implied they'd long since left their previous identities behind. "I thought they were… inhuman."

"They are," Mum said. "But they have individual identities and personalities like the rest of us do, and they're perfectly capable of holding grudges."

"Oh." *Oh.* Grandma's legion of enemies didn't just include humans. She'd clearly angered some demons too. "Do the Henbanes know that? Is that why they summoned that particular demon?"

"Now you're asking the right questions," Grandma said. "The answer is I don't know. The Henbanes are ignorant fools, so I'm inclined to think they picked that demon by complete accident."

"They still got two people killed," I said. "If I was the original target… I guess it explains why they went after Dad, but why'd they bother summoning a demon that's afraid of my sceptre?"

"The Henbanes didn't know," Mum said. "That doesn't mean that their meddling is harmless, however."

We all swivelled towards the Henbanes' house, where the darkness swathing the garden appeared impenetrable. There was no telling what we might find on the other side, and while the demon would think twice about trying to possess me as long as I held the sceptre, that didn't mean it couldn't hurt people I cared about.

"Right." I stepped towards the fence, my sceptre held aloft so its purple glow shone against the gloom. "I'm going in."

"No." Ramsey stepped up beside me. "Wait for the Reaper to come back first."

"Now you're lecturing *me* about acting alone?"

I let the sceptre's light spill over the fence. The glow penetrated the darkness, revealing the closed back door of the Henbanes' headquarters, but the shadowy patch hovering over the garden remained intact.

"That's the afterworld. There's got to be a circle of sage around half the garden to keep it caged."

We'd have to climb over the fence to take it apart, and there was no telling what might jump out of the darkness to attack us if we did.

Mum took in a breath. "Robin, use the sceptre."

"To do what?" That darkness wasn't the result of any magic I knew of. "Is there a counter-spell?"

"Yes," Mum replied. "The afterworld isn't accessible to the average person without a powerful spell to keep the doors between worlds open, but your sceptre is equally strong, if not more so. Use a reversal spell."

A reversal spell. That was one of the spells my grandmother had had me practise a thousand times, but I'd never used it to reverse a spell that opened the door to the afterworld before. If this went wrong…

"Go on," said Ramsey. "It's worth trying."

Coming from him, that was positively encouraging. Bolstered, I held up the glowing sceptre. "All right."

I concentrated hard as I waved the sceptre, and a current of light flooded the garden next to ours. *Whoa.* My vision blurred, the light too dazzling for me to keep my eyes open, and while I heard someone scream, the glare pushed on my eyelids and prevented me from seeing who.

When the glare dimmed, I risked opening my eyes a little. The darkness had vanished as if swept away, and the Henbane Coven's garden was deserted. No demons, no afterworld, but no sign of the culprit either.

"Did they go back into the house?" I stood on tiptoe, but I'd need to climb onto the fence to be able to see properly.

"If I were them, I'd escape into the forest instead."

Ramsey began to walk down the lawn towards the maze that concealed the gate connecting the garden to the woodland path, and I followed him.

Mum and Seth joined us as we walked through the maze and into the forest. The Ghasts had left a trail of broken branches in their wake, but I didn't see the summoner... or anyone else.

"The demon had better not have gone after Dad again." I turned left down the woodland path, wishing I had Maura's shadow-hopping power on my side.

Where is she? Did the demon give her the slip?

"I sent Tansy to warn him, but I haven't seen her since."

Maura would be hiding, if she had any sense.

As the others moved to follow me, I held out a hand to stop them. "Wait. You know the demon can possess any of you, but it's scared of the sceptre."

"That's a risk I'm willing to take," Ramsey said tightly. "Mother—I'll go with Robin. You should stay here with Seth and wait for the police."

I might have argued with him, but I was too interested to see how Mum reacted to him giving her orders.

Her lips pursed. "I don't think so. If you intend to accompany Robin, so will I."

This wasn't going to end well, but we didn't have time to argue, so I took the lead. It wasn't long before someone else walked onto the path—but it wasn't the summoner. Aunt Shannon faced us, an inhuman presence watching from the dark pits that had replaced her irises.

Oh. That's where the demon went.

"Wow," I said. "Dare I say it, but that's an improvement."

"You." Her voice sounded the same, but there was no mistaking the chilling tone of the demon. "You're Willow Wildwood's replacement."

"You're the demon who has a grudge against Grandma, are you?" I might have asked how my grandmother had managed to make an enemy of one of the most powerful beings in the afterworld, but I was more concerned with how it'd possessed my aunt. "How'd you shake off the Reaper?"

In answer, Aunt Shannon lunged forward, aiming at Mum and Ramsey. I waved the sceptre, instinctively, without thinking of what spell I wanted to use. The sceptre responded by unleashing a jet of purple light that sent my aunt crashing into a tree. In other circumstances, I would have found it satisfying to watch, but dread curled in my chest when the demon landed on its feet and smiled with my aunt's mouth.

"You're untrained," Aunt Shannon's voice said. "Despite the power of that instrument in your hands, you are not as skilled as its previous owner."

"Hey!" Maura appeared in a shadowy blur and swung a fist at Aunt Shannon.

Darkness enfolded Maura's hand, and this time my aunt staggered under the force of the hit. A shadowy form detached itself from her body—

"Not so fast." Maura leapt at the shadow and tackled it as if it were as solid as any of us.

The demon shrieked and writhed, but Maura gripped it with both hands, her fingers grasping its shadowy form.

"You're persistent, aren't you?" she puffed out, wrestling the figure to the ground. "Get into the afterworld."

Behind her, I glimpsed movement amid the trees. Someone fleeing. *The summoner.*

"Robin, where are you going?" Mum called to me.

"I'm going to find the summoner." I took off at a run, Ramsey on my heels, my gaze fixed on the trees where the figure had vanished. "Before they escape."

Nobody could traverse the Wildwood on foot, but if the summoner used a transportation spell, even the police wouldn't be able to catch up to them without knowing their destination.

Upon glimpsing the figure ahead of me again, I picked up speed. "Hey, you!"

To my surprise, the summoner slowed her sprint, and when she revealed her face, I skidded to a halt.

"*Leona?*"

Her mouth twisted, and she lifted a hand. To my shock, my feet—and Ramsey's too— left the ground, as if an invisible force flung us backwards. The sceptre flew from my grip, landing in the bushes, and I crashed onto my back, winded. Not to mention confused.

Leona can't use magic. Can she?

"You," Ramsey said, lifting his head. "You're the magical dud. What did you do?"

"I made a deal." Blackness bled into Leona's eyes, and she gave the slightest smile when I lifted my head.

She's possessed too. And she'd disarmed me. "You… you do realise the demon will kill you, don't you?"

The demon evidently didn't need to feed on anyone—yet —but Leona was a walking target, whatever powers it had given her. I tried to rise, but shadowy magic engulfed her palm, and an invisible force pushed me down. *Damn.* As long as I didn't have my sceptre, I couldn't fight back.

"Gangway!" In a blur of red, Tansy dropped from a tree and landed on Leona's head.

Leona staggered, even the demon not knowing how to respond to a surprise squirrel attack, and I seized my chance to dive into the bushes where my sceptre had fallen.

Ramsey lifted his wand first, knocking Leona off her feet. Tansy remained clinging to her head, claws digging in, and Leona screamed. If she could feel pain, the demon wasn't completely in control of her, but she flailed her hands and dislodged Tansy from her face.

My fingers closed around the sceptre as Leona pulled out her own wand.

"Stop!" I shouted.

Too late. A flash of light engulfed witch and demon both, and they vanished. I lowered the sceptre, and Maura came running into view.

"Who was that?"

"The summoner was possessed—they made a deal." I gestured at the spot where Leona had vanished, while Tansy came scurrying to my side. "She used a transportation spell… I don't know where she went."

"She won't last a day," Maura said. "Especially if she's as weak as you said."

That was not as reassuring as I might have hoped. "That means the demon will be on the loose among humans. And—it knew me. So did the demon that possessed my aunt."

"Interesting," Maura said. "Your grandmother must have had a hell of a career as Head Witch if she angered at least two demons."

"No kidding." I looked for Ramsey and saw him talking to Mum, who'd caught up to us. Grandma, however, must have been back at headquarters. "I wish she'd *told* me."

Was this what her training had been leading up to? The demon had said that I wasn't strong enough yet, and the fact that Leona had been able to disarm me proved that, but Maura wouldn't be able to stay here forever. If the demon came back… or if someone else summoned its friend… *we're in trouble.*

The sceptre glowed in my hand, and I knew with a rush of certainty that this was why it had chosen me as its wielder.

My purpose as Head Witch was to banish Grandma's demons.

16

My office was not the ideal place for a family gathering, but that's where we all ended up. Including my dad, who'd come straight here after he'd called me to confirm the demon was gone. I'd said I'd explain in person, but I hadn't expected him to end up awkwardly crammed into my office along with Ramsey, Mum, Chloe, Maura, and me.

Not to mention Tansy, who perched on Chloe's desk, next to Carmilla. I was certain Grandma's familiar was only pretending to be asleep, just like I knew that Grandma herself was listening to every word we spoke from her hiding place in the afterworld.

"We need to find that missing book," I said—mostly to Mum and Ramsey. "Are you sure Leona took it with her?"

"My officers haven't found anything yet," Ramsey said, "and the other members of the Henbane Coven claimed that Leona didn't come back into the building before she fled."

"She came back long enough to set up a summoning spell on the lawn," I remarked. "I find it hard to believe that they were completely ignorant of what she was doing."

"It's possible, if Tiffany was the one who trained her," Chloe ventured. Once she'd got over her initial shock, she'd jumped straight into her seat and opened her laptop to start putting together my official statement to the coven. "Head Witch, do you want me to mention the book?"

"No, and I told you that you don't have to do that now."

I'd have sat at my own desk, but it was currently occupied by Maura. She claimed to be fatigued from battling the demons, which was fair, and had slumped down amid my paperwork. At least her ghostly brother hadn't come along too.

"The coven will expect a statement," Mum said to me.

"They should have been here themselves," said Dad, causing everyone to stare at him as if they'd forgotten he was in the room. He hadn't been in the Wildwood headquarters for a long time, and he looked less than comfortable in my office. "Aren't they supposed to back up the Head Witch?"

"Yes, they are," I said, cutting through Mum's protest. "Aunt Shannon was the only person except Mum who showed her face, and she ran away. Then she got herself possessed, which serves her right if you ask me."

"Really, Robin." Mum clucked her teeth. "My sister had an unpleasant shock."

"Good." I didn't care if the woman herself was listening in —she'd done nothing but hinder me in my attempts to track down the demon and hadn't been of any use whatsoever in the end. "Don't worry, I won't mention her attempt to run away in my speech to the council."

I had to talk to the police, too, though Ramsey's officers were currently running around the Henbanes' base looking for more evidence—the ones who weren't searching the forest for Leona, of course. The odds of them finding her were low, but there was a possibility she would come back for me if her demon asked.

As for Maura, she looked on the verge of passing out, but she was also the only witness for parts of the fight, and Mum had refused to let her go back to the inn.

"I don't understand why these demons are fixated on Robin," said Dad.

"Grandma," I answered. "She did something to tick them off, and since demons can't die, they've been hanging around in the afterworld holding a grudge for years. Right, Mum?"

She grimaced. "Yes, but it was many decades ago that my mother first encountered them."

"That's no excuse for her not to tell me," I said. "They were waiting right there in the afterworld for someone to summon them, and they were prepared to target all our family members, even the non-witches."

Dad shifted on his feet, self-consciously. "If this Leona is still somewhere in the forest, I'll have to tell Jessica if it's no longer safe for us to live there."

"It won't make a difference whether you live in the forest or not, if the demon has you marked," said Mum. "There are ways to protect your house and your family without needing to move."

"Sage," I said at once. "I'll cover the place in the stuff."

"Absolutely not." Grandma appeared amid the filing cabinets, where I'd suspected she was hiding. "I won't have that foul stuff in here."

"You're the one who ticked off two demons—and that's just the ones I know about," I said. "How do I know you aren't hiding anything else?"

"She's right." Maura sat upright, her face paler than usual but her gaze steady when she addressed my grandmother's ghost. "And don't look at me like that. I'm not in your family. I don't have to show you respect."

"You do if you don't want me to report you as a rogue." Grandma gave Maura a wicked smile. "I'll have you know I met the local Reapers while I was alive. Who do you think helped me deal with my little demon problem?"

Maura glowered back at her. "Can you guarantee the same Reapers would help you twice? I was going to offer to come back if you need a hand, but if you'd rather I didn't..."

"You don't have to," I said.

Maura had her own life to go back to, and I couldn't keep her on as a bodyguard in case the demon possessing Leona came back. No. I had to learn to deal with the demon myself. Somehow.

"As the demons' *current* target, I have the right to a full explanation, Grandma. If you'd rather talk to me alone, we can do that later, but you can't wriggle out of this one. Whether Leona survives or not, those demons will be back for me."

"How can she have been possessed?" Chloe asked tremulously. "She has no magic."

"Someone without magic can still be possessed," Maura said. "If I had to guess, she had a friend do the actual summoning. Though now that she has a book with the proper instructions, I bet she'll be on the lookout for more allies."

"Thanks to Tiffany." I met Ramsey's eyes and was surprised at the fury in his expression. "What was that you said about moving her to a more secure prison?"

"I'll deal with her myself, after we've weeded out Leona's accomplices."

"I'd dismantle the whole Henbane Coven, personally," Maura said. "Wouldn't be the first time."

"No wonder the coven didn't like you," Tansy remarked.

I decided against translating my familiar's words for Maura's benefit. "Dad—if you need anything, let me know. I can help protect you and your family."

When Mum made to speak, I gave her a warning look,

telling her not to argue. There were some things that were not negotiable.

"I—I'll have to talk to Jessica." He ducked his head, shuffling towards the door. "If you're sure that *thing* isn't going to come back."

"Not with the coven on full alert," Mum said crisply, without making eye contact with him. "She'll be lying low—and if the Reaper is right, the demon will feed on her soon."

"Then it'll have to find a new host," I surmised. "Maura, is it at all possible to kill a demon?"

"No," said Maura. "I mean, you can banish it deeper into the afterworld, but it'll keep coming back. They're immortal."

"And a massive pain." I swivelled to my grandmother's ghost. "Why did you have to make an enemy of the one magical being that can't be killed?"

"I banished them for two decades!" she scoffed. "I expected gratitude, not accusations."

"You're the one who banished them?" Maura raised a brow at her. "That explains the personal nature of their grudge."

"Two decades," I repeated. If I did the same, it would at least ensure they didn't bother my family for the duration of my time as Head Witch. "How'd they escape?"

"They're crafty," Maura answered. "I don't have full knowledge, but I'd guess that every time someone summons anything from the afterworld, it weakens the chains on the demons banished to the deeper regions."

"Tiffany's fault, then." Along with everything else. "Did *she* know our family's history with the demons?"

"She might have," said Mum. "Whether she told Leona or not remains to be seen."

"I bet she did," I said. "They made a deal after they found common ground. Namely, their mutual grudge against our coven."

It was hard *not* to apply part of the blame to Grandma, especially now that I knew this was the reason I'd been chosen by the sceptre to begin with.

The office door nudged inward, and Seth peered in. "We have the suspects—two witches who admitted to helping Leona—in custody, but we didn't find the book."

"Leona must have taken it," said Ramsey. "I thought so."

Would Leona survive? Her lack of magic worked against her, and the demon needed to feed on life energy too. They wouldn't find much of that in the Wildwood.

Whether she survived or not, though, the demon would endure. When it came back, I had to be ready.

———

Maura had paid for one more night at the Owl's Nest, so she and her brother accompanied me to the pub again that evening. We were joined by Rowan and Piper—and Harvey, who'd shown up on the doorstep to my mother's house shortly after I'd finally got home from the office.

"Your grandmother has gone too far this time," said Piper from across the table. She'd warmed up to Maura considerably after learning she'd helped save all our necks from the demon. "What reason did she give for not telling you she was on two demons' hit lists?"

I sipped my cocktail—I didn't normally drink on a work evening, but I'd earned it. "She banished them into the afterworld for two decades. Which proves it can be done, if nothing else."

"Still," Harvey said. "She willingly endangered your life—not to mention everyone close to you."

"I know." I put down my glass, acutely aware that three of the people I cared most about in the world were right here with me. "I wish I could hunt her down myself."

"No," said Rowan. "It'll get you killed."

"I'm not actually going after her," I amended. "I don't even know where she is, and the demon is scared enough of my sceptre to stay away. For now."

"Yeah," said Maura. "You need to contact your local Reapers, in my opinion. Not sure if they'd be willing to help out twice, but they listened to your grandmother once before."

"Believe me, it's on the list."

I had to admit I didn't know how I felt about Maura leaving town. Demon aside, she'd certainly made for a memorable weekend—as had her brother, who was currently tap-dancing above the bar without a care for our serious conversation.

"I'm not going to force you to help me out again, don't worry," I said to Maura.

"Are you sure you don't want me to exorcise that trouble-some ghost in your office?"

"Tempting." I tried for a light tone, but Harvey's concerned expression sobered me. "No. This is her mess, and she's going to help me clean it up."

That I'd make sure of.

———

The following day, Mum gave me the morning off after I gave my announcement to the rest of the coven. Unusual, though the meeting itself was as uncomfortable as I'd expected. The coven was in too much shock to give me grief over my unrehearsed and blunt speech, though, and even Aunt Shannon had been unusually quiet since recovering from being possessed. An improvement, but it wouldn't last.

After leaving the office, I went to say goodbye to Maura and Mart. The latter had made no apologies for hiding in his room while the rest of us had run the risk of danger, but frankly there wasn't much he could have done against the demon. In any case, the forest was back to normal, and the abundance of birds for Tansy to chase out of the trees proved Leona and her demon were far away from here.

"You don't need me to detect demons for you if your familiar can do it instead," Maura remarked when I pointed this out. "Animals are more sensible than people."

"That I agree on," I said. "Ah—do you have any tips for me on how to convince the other Reapers to help with our little demon problem?"

"Try not to mention my name," she said. "They're stringent rule-followers, and some of them would peg me as a rogue even when it's technically not true."

"They're also boring," Mart added.

That figured. "I won't say a word. I guess I'll have to tell them I got lucky and drove away the demon by throwing sage at Leona."

"Speaking of which, I can smell it on you."

"Right." I reached into my pocket. "I'm going to douse my dad's entire house in it. At least he doesn't have any resident ghosts who'd kick up a fuss like Grandma would."

"I wouldn't blame you for wanting to give her the boot, but I guess you need her help," Maura said.

"Unfortunately." Grandma and I were at odds, but she was the one in charge of my training, and I had to tolerate her for as long as necessary. "She's still finding ways to surprise me from beyond the grave, I'll say that much for her."

"Pretty standard for a ghost." Maura waved a hand, and shadows swept around her feet.

I hadn't expected her to walk through the whole forest without using a short cut, but the sight of the shadows made me shiver at the reminder of the close call we'd had. The birdsong quieted, and Tansy hopped out of her tree and sat on my shoulder. Despite myself, my fingers tightened around the sceptre, my heartbeat quickening.

"Relax, it's quiet over here," Maura said, seeing my reaction. "If you need me, give me a shout."

"Sure." I raised a hand in farewell.

She and Mart both vanished, along with the shadows. A moment later, the birdsong started again as if it had never stopped, and the forest was tranquil once more.

"She's not as bad as I thought, but I'm not sorry this is over." Tansy buried her head in my hair. "I wish they'd taken that demon with them."

"Wouldn't we be so lucky."

I turned my attention back to the path, ready to walk the rest of the way to Dad's house, and I did a double take when Ramsey stepped into view from behind a tree.

"She's gone?" He indicated the spot where Maura had vanished.

"Yeah, but I have her number if I need to call her." I lowered the sceptre. "What're you doing here? Looking for Leona?"

"No." He took a breath. "Did you bring sage with you?"

"Yes… Why?" Then it clicked. *Had he come to help Dad and Jessica?* "I thought you'd be at the office."

"I won't be able to stay for long, but I wanted to help."

"Dad will be happy to see you."

He grunted in acknowledgement, his face slightly red. I fell into step with him, savouring the quiet of the forest and the birdsong in the air—and the knowledge that despite the challenge ahead of us, change wasn't impossible. Even for my family.

ABOUT THE AUTHOR

Elle Adams lives in the middle of England, where she spends most of her time reading an ever-growing mountain of books, planning her next adventure, or writing. Elle's books are humorous mysteries with a paranormal twist, packed with magical mayhem.

She also writes urban and contemporary fantasy novels as Emma L. Adams.

Visit http://www.elleadamsauthor.com/ to find out more about Elle's books.

www.ingramcontent.com/pod-product-compliance
Lightning Source LLC
Chambersburg PA
CBHW020816190726
48285CB00006B/2302